CLAIMED BY HER
BILLIONAIRE
PROTECTOR

CLAIMED BY HER BILLIONAIRE PROTECTOR

ROBYN DONALD

MILLS & BOON

First published in Great Britain 2018
by Mills & Boon, an imprint of HarperCollins*Publishers*
1 London Bridge Street, London, SE1 9GF

Large Print edition 2018

© 2018 Robyn Donald Kingston

ISBN: 978-0-263-07392-8

MIX
Paper from
responsible sources
FSC™ C007454

This book is produced from independently certified
FSC™ paper to ensure responsible forest management.
For more information visit www.harpercollins.co.uk/green.

Printed and bound in Great Britain
by CPI Group (UK) Ltd, Croydon, CR0 4YY

3478216-8

For Sheila,
who patiently waited a long time for this one!

Many thanks for everything.

CHAPTER ONE

NIKO RADCLIFFE HAD expected an unsophisticated band playing unsophisticated country music. After all, this was the northernmost part of New Zealand, a farming region of small villages, ancient volcanoes and stunning coastal scenery. Narrow and sea-bordered, the peninsula thrust north towards the equator, relying on its beauty and its history to attract tourists.

So the strains of mellow jazz drifting across the car park as he walked towards Waipuna Hall came as a pleasant surprise. Either the Far North had an unusually professional musical culture, or—more likely—the committee who'd organised the Waipuna Centennial Ball had hired the band from Auckland.

At the doors a middle-aged man stepped towards him. 'Good evening. Can I see your ticket, please?'

Niko held it out, and after a quick scan the doorman nodded and said, 'Welcome to Waipuna, Mr Radcliffe. I hope you enjoy the evening.'

Niko had his doubts about that, but he said, 'Thank you,' and walked into the hall, stopping just inside the doors to survey the crowd.

The district had done the occasion proud. Garlands of flowers looped around the walls, their faint evocative perfume floating on the warm air. Men in the stark black and white of evening dress steered partners clad in a multitude of colours. Everyone appeared to be having a fine time.

Whoever had done the decorations had talent, and must have denuded quite a few farm and village gardens of flowers. Their soft, fresh perfume hung in the warm air, the blooms competing in colour with the women's bright copies of Twenties' flapper fashions.

Idly, Niko allowed his eyes to follow one of the dancers. Although she had her back to him, she was above average height, and her sleek head of strawberry-blonde hair made her easy to see amongst the dancers. Her grace should have won her a better partner than the middle-aged man steering her somewhat clumsily through the crowd. When they turned Niko recognised him—

Bruce Nixon, husband of the woman who headed the Waipuna Centenary Ball committee.

The music stopped, the floor began to empty, and the noise changed to a buzz of chatter and laughter. His gaze still held by that bright crown of hair, Niko realised the woman and her partner were walking towards Mrs Nixon, the only other person in the hall he recognised. In spite of his unexpected arrival in Waipuna several days previously she'd tracked him down and welcomed him to the Far North.

'And as the new owner of Mana Station it would be appreciated if you could come to our Hall Centennial Ball and meet some of the local people,' she'd told him, her tone reminding him of his rather severe first governess.

He'd agreed to endure the possible boredom of a country ball because his purchase of the cattle station had been a matter of comment in the national media, quite a bit of it critical. The new manager he'd appointed had also informed him of discontent caused by yet another foreign absentee owner buying up a large agricultural holding in New Zealand.

Especially an owner with his background. The only child of a European aristocrat who'd fallen crazily in love with a rugged New Zealander, Niko could barely recall his early life on his father's vast tussock-clad hill station in the South Island. He'd been just five years old when his mother had fled with him back to her father's palace in San Mari, a small European principality.

So it was logical enough for him to be considered a foreigner. The fact that he'd forged an empire for himself in commerce wasn't likely to cut much ice—if any—with pragmatic, farming Kiwis.

Given time, they'd discover that he was nothing like the previous owner of Mana Station, who'd not only stripped the station of every available cent for years, eventually bringing what had once been a profitable farming concern so close to ruin that he'd been forced to sell, but had appointed an inefficient, corrupt farm manager.

Doubtless Niko's dismissal of that man would cause more gossip.

Mrs Nixon looked across the hall, saw him, and smiled, beckoning him across. Noting wryly that he was being openly inspected by at least half of the dancers, Niko set off towards her.

The strawberry blonde could be Mrs Nixon's daughter, although that seemed unlikely. Both

Mrs Nixon and her husband were short and rather stout, whereas the redhead was slender.

Niko's gaze narrowed as he took in the younger woman's face—fine features and ivory skin, faintly flushed with exertion. Her violet silk shift subtly revealed soft curves and long limbs. She wasn't beautiful, yet something about her stirred his blood. Her hair was pulled back from her face and confined in a knot at the base of her neck. Ivory-skinned, she turned her head slightly as he walked towards them, revealing slightly tilted eyes and a full, sensuous mouth.

'Mr Radcliffe! I'd begun to think you weren't coming!' Mrs Nixon beamed as he arrived.

'I'm sorry I'm late,' he said smoothly. 'Your ball is obviously a huge success.'

Her smile widened even further. 'I hope you enjoy it. You've met my husband, Bruce, of course.'

While the two men shook hands, she went on, 'And this is Elana Grange, who helped us enormously with the organisation for tonight, and also with the decorations. She's a neighbour of yours—right next door at Anchor Bay, in fact.' The smile she directed at her companion was almost mischievous. 'Elana, this is Niko Radcliffe, the new owner of Mana Station.'

'How do you do, Mr Radcliffe.'

Her voice was cool, and so was the hand she extended, allowed to lie in his for a brief moment, and then retrieved.

For the length of a heartbeat, Niko's initial awareness gave way to a sensation infinitely more primal—a swift, uncontrollable physical response that startled him. Elana Grange radiated a subtly provocative allure that roused him in a way he hadn't experienced before.

Yet he sensed contradictions. Slightly tilted eyes of dark green speckled with gold gave her an exotic air, but her level gaze lacked the coquettish awareness he often saw in women's eyes. And although her mouth hinted at passion, something about the lift of her square chin indicated a controlled reserve.

Which could, of course, be deliberate. Several bitter experiences in his youth had led to a sardonic appreciation of the various methods of feminine provocation. If Elana Grange expected him to be intrigued by her aloofness, she'd discover she was wrong. Niko had learned to deal with women who viewed him either as a challenge, or a path to social and material advancement.

Her sophisticated appearance was completely at odds with the dilapidated little shack she lived in, huddled just outside the gates to Mana Station. He'd noticed it from the helicopter as he'd arrived at Mana homestead, and assumed the place was a ruin. Judging by the state of the roof, its owner was going to face a large repair bill some time soon.

Mrs Nixon said enthusiastically, 'I'm so glad you could make it tonight, Mr Radcliffe. Or should I call you Count?'

'No. My name is Niko.'

Another slight smile curved Elana Grange's soft mouth. It gave her a fey look, an air of cool mystery that summoned another swift, startlingly carnal response in Niko.

Mrs Nixon smiled. 'Very well, *Niko.*' She glanced at the woman beside her. 'Elana was just wondering why you'd chosen to buy Mana Station when it's almost derelict.'

A faint colour warmed the face of the woman beside her. Embarrassed she might be, Niko thought cynically, but his answer would almost certainly be circulated through the district. So he told her the truth. 'I spent my early years on a high country station in the South Island, as well as some school holidays, and developed an affection for New Zealand and its stunning countryside. As for Mana—it needs rescuing.'

An interesting and unexpected comment, Elana decided. However, his purchase of the large sheep and cattle station had caused quite a lot of publicity, and he was probably aware that not all of it had been favourable. Pretending to an affection for the country could be a way to alleviate that.

The Count had an interesting voice, if you liked men's voices deep with a hard edge. He'd judged his handshake perfectly—strong enough to be masterful without causing pain. Once he'd released her hand she'd had to stop herself from rubbing her tingling palm surreptitiously against her side.

Her first glance at the arrogant jut of his jaw had set every warning instinct on full alert. And the unsparing assessment of his ice-blue gaze had reinforced her surge of defensiveness. It was highly unlikely she'd ever become friends with the new owner of Mana Station.

However, her foolish body was buzzing with

sensual excitement. His lean, charismatic muscularity emphasised by wide shoulders and his height, Count Niko Radcliffe wore his formal evening clothes with an intimidating confidence that was like nothing she'd seen before.

Cool it, Elana commanded her jumping heartbeat. Handsome men were not that uncommon, and she'd seen enough photographs of him in the media to know what to expect.

But photographs failed to convey his effortless air of authority or the powerful aura that was more than physical, backed by a disturbing smile. According to the media he ran his numerous interests with a formidable combination of intelligence, determination and ruthlessness.

An image formed in her mind of some warrior king of long ago, one who ruled by sheer force of character.

Chemistry, she decided, trying to dampen her foolish reaction with irony. Some men had it in spades. And dangerously attractive though he seemed, Niko Radcliffe's magnetism owed nothing to honesty or kindness or—well, any of the virtues.

But then, royal billionaires probably didn't need honesty or kindness to attract some women.

Immediately ashamed of the snide thought, she banished it. According to Mrs Nixon, an avid reader of gossip magazines, he chose lovers noted for their beauty and intelligence, the latest one a gorgeous English aristocrat.

And in farming circles he had a good reputation. Only a few weeks ago she'd read an article about his rescue of the sheep and cattle station he'd inherited from his father. He'd spent much money killing the wilding pines that threatened to turn the land into forest, and clearing the station of goats. Apparently he was determined to clear it of rabbits too, although he'd admitted he might need a miracle for that.

She risked a swift upwards glance, her pulse speeding as her eyes clashed with his. Somehow she just couldn't see this man, completely assured in his perfectly tailored evening clothes, shooting goats or hauling out pine seedlings.

Ah well, no doubt he had minions to do the heavy work.

Fixing a noncommittal smile to her lips, she said lightly, 'Welcome to Northland, Mr Radcliffe.'

Black brows lifted. 'Niko,' he repeated with a

crisp intonation that came close to curtness. But then he smiled.

Elana was shocked by a fierce awareness that tightened her nerves and sinews. That smile was *something*!

And no doubt he was aware of its impact.

He added, 'Congratulations on the decorations. They are superb.'

Striving to control a swift surge of adrenalin, she forced herself to concentrate on his accent. He sounded almost English, but his faint foreign intonation no doubt came from his upbringing in a European palace.

Elana steadied her voice enough to say, 'Thank you—we had an excellent committee to work with.'

The band struck an imperative chord, and once the chatter faded the MC—a local farmer—spoke into the microphone, welcoming the crowd. Something far too close to relief gripped Elana when the man beside her turned to listen.

Stop being an idiot, she told herself robustly. OK, so the new owner of Mana had the kind of presence that attracted eyes and attention.

Definitely an alpha male—uncompromising and intolerant and intimidating.

Like her father. Just the sort of man she despised.

And feared...

The MC announced the next dance, and the Count turned to Mrs Nixon with a request that summoned a slight flush to her cheeks. 'Dear man, that's lovely of you, but I'm not dancing tonight. I managed to twist my ankle yesterday,' she said.

Horrified, Elana realised that Niko had no polite way out of asking her to dance.

Sure enough, he turned to her, hard eyes veiled by lashes too long for any man. 'May I have the pleasure?'

Say no.

But that would be ludicrous. After all, it was only one dance...

Her smile hiding, she fervently hoped, her abrupt and unwarranted reaction, she placed her fingers gingerly on his outstretched arm.

'So you live above Anchor Bay,' he said as the band struck up a tune. His tone indicated that he wasn't particularly interested.

Matching it, she answered, 'Yes.'

'You must be able to see quite a bit of Mana Station from there.'

'Yes.'

'You'll notice quite a few changes soon.'

Strangely, the purposeful note in his voice chilled her. She looked up, and for a couple of seconds their eyes locked. Blinking, she lowered her lashes against the ironic challenge in his cold blue gaze.

Suavely he asked, 'You're surprised?'

He saw too much. Elana struggled for something banal and conventional to say, but only managed, 'No.' When his brows drew together she added, 'I'm pleased. It's time someone gave Mana back some pride.'

He nodded. 'Exactly what I intend to do. Don't worry, I won't bore you with farming talk. Let's dance.'

A shiver ghosted the length of her spine as she stepped closer. For a foolish moment she felt she'd taken a forbidden step into an alternative world.

A dangerous world, she realised as they began to move together—a world where the rules no longer applied. Jumping heartbeats took her by surprise and her nostrils flared at the faint, exciting, potently male scent of him and the hard strength in the arms that imprisoned her.

Imprisoned her?

What a ridiculous thought!

Yet the heat of Niko Radcliffe's hand at her waist was stirring a blatant response. Her dress seemed suddenly far too revealing, the violet silk slithering over acutely sensitised skin in a sensuous massage.

Of course he danced superbly; she was ready to bet that lean, splendidly physical body would do anything well, from dancing to making love.

'Are you all right?'

His voice startled her. She had to swallow before she could speak and even then, she sounded hesitant. 'Yes, I'm fine.' A swift defiance made her glance up to meet hooded, glinting eyes. 'Why?'

'You seem a little tense,' he responded coolly, blue gaze unreadable. 'I rarely bite, and when I do, it's not to hurt.'

Heat zinged from her scalp to her toes, lighting fires all the way. That instinctive awareness strengthened into a sensation much more intense, so fiercely tantalising it shocked her.

Was he coming on to her?

No sooner had the thought flashed across her mind than she dismissed it. Of course he wasn't flirting! It was impossible to imagine Count Niko

Radcliffe doing anything so frivolous. So was he testing her?

If so, it was unkind. He was as out of place in Waipuna as she'd be in the rarefied social circles that were his natural habitat. According to Mrs Nixon, gorgeous film stars fell in love with him...

And probably the occasional princess. Gorgeous too, no doubt.

She couldn't care less, she thought sturdily, trying to corral her rampaging senses.

'So you're quite safe,' he drawled.

The note of mockery in his voice stiffened her spine. 'I'm always glad to have that assurance,' she retorted.

'Even when you don't necessarily believe it?'

Elana tried to come up with some innocuous answer, but before anything came to mind he continued curtly, 'Whatever you might have heard about me, I don't attack women.'

As soon as the words left his mouth Niko wondered why he'd said them. He spent more time fending off women than reassuring them of his integrity.

He had no illusions about the reason behind that sort of feminine interest. Money and power talked, and for a certain type of woman it was enough to seduce. Yet for some reason the note in Elana Grange's voice had struck a nerve.

Actually, *she* struck a nerve.

When they'd been introduced he'd noticed her fingers, long and slender and bare of rings, and for a moment he'd wondered what they'd feel like on his skin. And as she'd stepped into his arms, his whole body had tightened in swift, primitive response.

However, elegant though she appeared, he suspected Elana Grange wasn't sophisticated enough for the sort of relationships he chose. His affairs—nowhere near as many as suggested in gossip columns—had always been between two people who both liked and wanted each other, whose minds meshed. He valued intelligence as much as he did sex appeal.

And because he drew the line at breaking hearts, his lovers had always understood that he wasn't offering marriage.

Whatever sort of mind Elana Grange had, she looked like a dream—and danced like one too, her grace fulfilling the promise of her sinuous body.

Elana broke the silence between them. 'Mr Radcliffe, there have been rumours that you plan to develop Mana Station. Is that true?'

'What do you mean by *develop*?'

Wishing she'd stayed silent, she told him. 'Cut it into blocks, sell them off and make a gated community of it—'

'No,' he interrupted curtly. 'I'm planning to bring it back into the vital, productive station it once must have been.'

She couldn't stop herself from asking, 'Why?'

Broad shoulders lifting, he said, 'I despise waste. In San Mari every acre of land is precious, cherished and nurtured over the centuries, treated with respect. All agricultural and pastoral land should be viewed like that.' His tone altered as he finished, 'And call me Niko.'

Hoping no sign of her reluctance showed in her tone, she said, 'Then you must call me Elana.'

He laughed. Surprised, she glanced up, meeting his gaze with raised brows.

'Don't look so startled,' he said. 'When I came back to New Zealand it took me a few weeks to understand that although most people here call each other by their first names, it didn't necessarily denote friendship.'

Elana had never previously pondered the intri-

cacies of New Zealand ways of addressing people. Perhaps he was interested because he'd grown
up in a royal household, where such things were
important?

Or perhaps not, she thought wryly. Probably
he was just filling in a boring experience with
smooth small talk.

She considered a moment before replying,
'You're probably right. I think it's a preliminary
to a possible friendship—addressing a person by
his or her first name is an indication that you feel
he or she might be someone you'd like, once you
get to know him or her better.'

'So if you decide you don't like me, you'll call
me Mr Radcliffe?'

Elana allowed herself a careful smile. 'I'd probably avoid you. That way I wouldn't have to ad-
dress you at all.'

'So if I notice you fleeing from me, I'll have to
accept that I've done something that's displeased
you.'

Bemused, Elana looked up. Their eyes met, and
another tantalising rush of adrenalin boosted her
pulse rate into overdrive. A point in his favour
was the dry amusement in his voice.

Not that it mattered what sort of person he was—or only so far as he was a neighbour.

'Actually, I'm not into fleeing,' she told him briskly. 'And we like to believe we're an egalitarian society. But—didn't I read that you're a New Zealander too?'

'I have dual citizenship,' he said levelly.

A swift change of direction startled Elana until she realised she was being skilfully steered around a jitterbugging pair in the centre of the floor.

'Wrong period,' Niko Radcliffe observed dryly. 'They should be doing the Charleston.'

She said, 'But they're good.' The words had barely been spoken when the young man missed a step and stumbled towards them.

Instantly her partner's arm tightened, forcing Elana against his steely strength so that she was held firmly for a few seconds against the powerful muscles of his thighs. Sensation, so intense and sensuous it drove the breath from her lungs, scorched through her in a delicious, dangerous conflagration.

Concentrate on dancing, blast you, she commanded her wayward body fiercely, pushing a wilful erotic image into the furthest reaches of her brain and trying to lock the door on it.

Suddenly dry-mouthed, she breathed, 'Thanks.'

'It was nothing.' His voice was cool and uninflected.

Clearly he wasn't suffering the same potent response. Indeed, his arm had loosened swiftly as though he found her sudden closeness distasteful.

Chilled, she had to swallow before she could say, 'Perhaps we should tell them that jitterbugging arrived some years after the Twenties.'

'They're enjoying themselves,' he said dismissively, then surprised her by asking, 'Are you the local florist?'

Elana hesitated. He sounded quite interested—which seemed unlikely. Perhaps faking interest when bored out of his mind was another talent developed in that princely court...

OK, concentrate on small talk now, she told herself. *Ignore those pulsating seconds when you were plastered against him, and something weird happened to you.*

Sedately she told him, 'I work part-time in the florist's shop in Waipuna.'

'Was that always your ambition?' he asked, almost as though he were interested.

'No.' After a second's pause she added, 'I'm a librarian and I used to work in Auckland, but a couple of years ago a family situation meant I had to come home to Waipuna.'

The family situation being the accident that had killed her stepfather and confined her mother to a wheelchair.

'So you decided to stay here.'

Elana glanced up and met a narrowed blue gaze. Another of those unnerving shivers chased down her spine. In a tone she didn't recognise, she said, 'Yes.'

'Is there no library in Waipuna?'

'Yes, run by volunteers. There's no need for a professional librarian.'

'Ah, I see. Do you enjoy working in the florist's shop?'

Surely he couldn't be interested in a small-town woman in the wilds of northern New Zealand? He didn't need to hear that, although she loved Waipuna, she missed the stimulation of her career in Auckland.

She evaded, 'I can't remember a time when I wasn't fascinated by flowers. My mother was a fantastic gardener and apparently from the time I could toddle I drove her crazy by picking any blooms—' She stopped abruptly. *Any blooms her mother had been allowed to cultivate.* 'Often before they'd opened out,' she finished.

He gave the big hall a quick survey. 'You clearly have a talent for arranging them. Mrs Nixon also mentioned that you wrote the booklet—a short history—of the hall. I haven't read it yet, but intend to.'

Elana flushed. 'I hope you find it interesting.'

'Are you a historian as well as a librarian?'

'I did a history degree,' she said.

And wasn't surprised when he asked, 'Why?'

'Because I'm interested in history.' She added, 'After that my stepfather insisted I take a business course.'

'Very sensible of your stepfather,' Niko Radcliffe said dryly. 'From your tone, I gather you didn't want to do it. Was he right to insist?'

Elana didn't like the way he emphasised the word *stepfather.* Steve had been as dear to her as any father could be—infinitely dearer than her own father. She said briskly, 'Yes, he was right. It's been very useful.'

Especially over the past couple of years, after a friend had asked her to tape her great-grandmother's reminiscences and transcribe them so they could be bound into a book to mark her hundredth birthday. Elana found the task absorbing, enjoyed the whole experience and had been astounded when her friend's family insisted on paying her for the time she'd spent.

Even more astonishing, word had got around the district, and soon she was repeating the process. Then the editor of the local weekly newspaper commissioned her to write articles on the history of the district. As she was working for only three days a week at the florist's shop, the money came in handy, and she loved the research.

To her relief the music drew to a close. Niko Radcliffe released her and offered an arm. Forcing herself to relax, she took it, trying to ignore the sudden chill aching through her—a bewildering sense of abandonment.

How could a man she'd only just met have that effect on her?

Be sensible, she told herself robustly as they walked across the hall towards Mr and Mrs Nixon. *So you're attracted to him? So what? You're probably not the only one here tonight to be so aware of him...*

Over the centuries women had learned to recognise an alpha male. For probably most of humankind's existence, a strong capable father to one's children gave them a much better chance of survival.

And, tall and good-looking, with that indefinable magnetism—not to mention the fact that he was rich, she thought sardonically—everything about him proclaimed Count Niko Radcliffe a member of that exclusive group.

Which was no reason to fantasise about feeling strangely at home in his arms. When the next dance was announced he'd choose a different woman to partner him, and that woman might well feel the same subliminal excitement, a reckless tug of sexuality both dangerous and compelling.

Together they walked to where the Nixons had just finished chatting to another couple. Acutely aware of sideways glances, Elana was surprised by an odd regret when they arrived.

Mrs Nixon observed, 'Good evasive action, Niko. For a second I thought we might need to call on my first-aid skills, but you saved the day with that sidestep. Young Hamish and his partner are going to have to practise jiving a bit longer before they're safe enough to do it in public.'

His smile held a tinge of irony. 'Fortunately I had an excellent partner.'

The older woman sighed. 'My grandmother was a great dancer—she could still do a mean Charleston when she was eighty, and her tales of balls and parties used to make me deeply envious. Then rock and roll came onto the scene when my parents were young. I always felt I missed out on being wild and rebellious.'

'Surely punk must have been wild and rebellious enough,' Elana teased.

Mrs Nixon chuckled. 'A bit too much for me, I'm afraid,' she confessed. 'And now I find I've turned into my father—when I hear the hit songs today I mutter about their lack of tune and how they don't sing clearly enough for me to understand the words.'

'Possibly a good thing,' Niko observed coolly. 'Tell me, why did the committee choose the Twenties as a theme for tonight? I believe the hall was built in the early twentieth century, so you should have been celebrating its centennial some years ago?'

Mrs Nixon smiled. 'Nobody was interested in running a ball to celebrate the centennial then, but a year ago a group of us decided Waipuna deserved a Centennial Ball. So we called it that. It meant that people who'd give an ordinary dance a miss came for it—some from overseas,' she finished proudly. 'It's been a lovely reunion.'

He laughed, and Elana's heart missed a beat. 'Good thinking. So why the Twenties theme?'

'Comfort.'

Brows lifting, he echoed, 'Comfort?'

'Comfort,' Mrs Nixon repeated firmly. 'In the early twentieth century women were still confined to elaborate clothes and corsets. We decided unanimously that comfort is more sensible than historical accuracy.'

'To every woman's relief,' Elana observed. 'As well, it's a lot easier to sew a Twenties shift than the gowns they wore twenty years previously.'

Niko glanced down, struck by the way the lights shimmered on her gleaming hair. Freed from the neat knot at the back of her neck it would look like silk. Into his mind sprang an image of the soft swathe spread out across a pillow—of her lithe, ivory-skinned body against white sheets, green-gold eyes heavy-lidded and beckoning...

Strange how exotic eyes and a fall of bright hair could lend spice to an occasion...

Irritated by a fierce surge of desire, he suppressed the tantalising thought and concentrated on the conversation.

He'd expected little entertainment from this evening. If his presence at the ball went some way to convincing the district that he intended to return Mana Station to full production again—which would mean jobs for local people—it would make the new manager's position easier.

Above the babble of conversation and laughter he discerned a rapidly approaching roar as some idiot drove past the hall, achieving as much noise as he could from a badly maintained engine.

When the noise had faded Mr Nixon told him laconically, 'One of the local hoons. Like all young kids with an attitude, they like to stir up the district periodically. No harm to them, by and large.'

Niko nodded. The band struck up for the next dance, and some young guy in evening clothes slightly too big for him came up and asked Elana Grange for it. Smiling up at him, she accepted.

Watching them dance, Niko resisted a swift emotion that veered dangerously close towards possessiveness. Startled by its intensity, he secured one of the matrons Mrs Nixon introduced him to, and guided her onto the floor. But although his partner was a brilliant dancer, and had a sharp, somewhat acerbic wit, he had to force himself to concentrate on her and not allow his gaze to follow Elana Grange around the room.

As the evening wore on he noted she was a popular dance partner, but seemed to favour no particular man, apparently enjoying her turns with middle-aged farmers as well as with younger men.

Keeping her eyes firmly away from Niko Radcliffe, Elana chatted with old friends and acquaintances, grateful that he didn't approach her for any more dances.

By the time midnight arrived she was strangely tired, but she managed to hide any yawns until she slid into her car, pulling out to follow his car. It suited him—big enough to be comfortable for a tall man, super-sophisticated yet tough…

Stop this right now, she told herself grimly. *You're being an idiot. OK, so he looks like some romantic fantasy, all strength and good looks and seething with charisma, but that's no reason for you to feel as though you've overdosed on champagne.*

Frowning ferociously, she stifled another yawn and concentrated on the road as it narrowed ahead. Some time during the ball it had rained and the tarseal shone slickly in the headlights. After a few kilometres the road swung towards the coast and the surface turned to gravel as it dived into the darkness of the tall kanuka scrub crowding the verges.

About halfway home, scarlet tail-lights ahead warned her of trouble. Slamming on her own brakes, she gasped as the seatbelt cut across her breasts.

When her stunned gaze discerned the cause of the sudden stop, she gulped, 'Oh, *no*—'

CHAPTER TWO

SHOCKINGLY, THE GLARE of the headlights revealed a stationary vehicle on its side. The driver had failed to take the corner and the car had skidded into the ditch before sliding along the clay bank that bordered the road on the passenger's side.

Hideous memories of another accident, the one that had killed her stepfather, and ultimately her mother, flashed through Elana's mind. Sick apprehension tightened her stomach and froze her thoughts into incoherence until she realised that Niko Radcliffe was already out of his vehicle and running towards the wreck.

Fingers shaking, she released her seatbelt and opened the door. Her first instinct was to join him, but second thoughts saw her haul the first-aid kit from the glove box.

Clutching it, she ran, heartbeats thudding in her ears as Niko wrenched open the driver's door and leaned inside.

'Oh, dear God, *please...*' Elana breathed a silent prayer that jerked to a sudden stop when she realised he was half inside the car, presumably undoing the driver's seatbelt.

Over his shoulder he commanded harshly, 'Get back. Quickly—I can smell petrol.'

So could she now, the acrid stench cutting through the minty perfume from the kanuka trees. At least the force of the collision had stopped the engine.

'Go,' Niko Radcliffe ordered, dragging the driver free of the car in one ferociously powerful movement.

'I'll help you—'

He broke in, 'Have you got a cell phone?'

'Yes, but—'

'Then get back to your car and use it to call for help.'

Torn between summoning the emergency services and helping him, Elana wavered.

'Move! And stay there!'

The peremptory command raised her hackles, but sent her running back. Snatching up her cell phone, she tapped out the emergency number, eyes fixed on Niko and his limp burden as he strode past his own vehicle towards her.

'Ambulance, fire engine and police,' she told the emergency operator, and answered the subsequent questions as clearly and concisely as she could, finishing by saying, 'The smell of petrol seems to be getting much stronger. I have to go now.'

She dropped the phone onto the driver's seat and ran towards Niko and his burden.

He had to be immensely strong, because, although the hard angles of his face were slick with sweat, he'd carried the driver of the wrecked car past their vehicles to what she fervently hoped was a safe distance.

Breathing heavily, he laid the unconscious man on the narrow, stony verge before straightening. 'How long will it take them to get here?'

'About fifteen minutes,' Elana told him unevenly, adding, 'I hope that not too many of the volunteers were drinking champagne at the ball.' She dropped to her knees beside the still—*dangerously* still—driver. 'Jordan,' she said urgently, groping for his wrist. 'Jordan, can you hear me? It's Elana Grange. Open your eyes if you can.'

'Who is he?'

'Jordan Cooper.' Tears clogged her eyes. 'He's only a kid—about eighteen.'

'Any pulse?'

Steady, she told herself when her probing fingers found nothing. *Concentrate.* 'No.'

Inwardly shaking, she explored a little further, and to her intense relief recognised the faint flutter of heartbeats against her fingers. 'Yes. He's alive.' *Barely...*

She laid a gentle hand on the driver's chest, some of her panic fading when she felt it rise and fall beneath her palm. 'He's breathing.'

'Keep checking. Tell me at once if his pulse stops or he stops breathing.'

Vowing to take the next first-aid course available, she infused her tone with a confidence she didn't feel. 'Jordan, hang on in there. You're going to be all right. Help is coming and will be here soon. Keep breathing.'

Did he hear her? Probably not, but that faint flutter steadied a little and his breathing became slightly less harsh.

Niko surveyed her, crouched on the stones, her long fingers clasping the unconscious man's wrist.

As though sheer willpower could keep him alive, she urged again, 'Keep breathing, Jordan, keep breathing. It won't be long now before the ambulance gets here.'

Never had time dragged so slowly. Niko hoped to heaven he hadn't made Jordan's injuries—whatever they were—worse by hauling him from the car. The boy had worn a seatbelt so he'd almost certainly have escaped severe injury, although to knock him out the car must have hit the bank heavily.

And the stench of spilt petrol hung in the cool air, a constant threat.

At last the silence, broken only by the regular mournful *morepork* call of a nearby owl and Elana's commands to Jordan to keep breathing, was interrupted by the sound of engines labouring up the hill.

Her head jerked up. Voice trembling with relief, she said, 'Jordan, the ambulance is almost here. I can see its lights flashing through the bush. Keep breathing. You're going to be all right.'

She fell silent as the ambulance arrived, followed closely by a fire engine and a police car.

Gladly handing over to those who knew what they were doing, Niko gave silent thanks for volunteers, and decided to double the donation he gave to each organisation.

Reaching down, he pulled Elana gently to her feet. Although she valiantly straightened her shoulders, she couldn't hide the shivers that wracked her slender body.

He shrugged out of his jacket and draped it across her shoulders. 'All right?'

'Yes.'

The quaver in her voice and the shiver that accompanied it told him she was in mild shock. Understandable, especially as she knew the kid.

He looped an arm around her shoulder. When she flinched he demanded, 'What's the matter? Did your seatbelt hurt you?'

'No.' She held herself stiffly while he urged her onto the side of the road out of the way of the vehicles. 'I'm all right.'

And presumably to prove it, she moved away from him, putting distance between them. For some reason that exasperated him. Eyes narrowed, he kept a close watch on her while the ambulance personnel got to work and what at first seemed chaos soon resolved itself into a well-oiled routine that swiftly transferred the still-unconscious youth to the ambulance.

'Elana?' A young policeman stopped in front of them, frowning. 'You all right?'

'Don't worry, Phil, I'm fine,' she said, and summoned a shaky smile.

'Rotten thing to happen to you—' He stopped, looking profoundly uncomfortable, then asked hastily, 'You sure you're OK?'

Niko glanced down at her. What was going on? Had she been involved in an accident recently?

'I'm fine,' she repeated, her voice a little firmer, and added, 'Truly, Phil, I'm all right.'

The young cop kept his gaze on her face. 'Can you tell me what happened?'

'Neither of us saw it,' Niko informed him. 'It looks as though he took the corner too fast, overcorrected, then hit the bank at speed. I think we got here almost immediately after that.'

Questions had to be asked and answered, Niko knew, but surely not now. The woman beside him was no longer shaking, but she was still in shock. No wonder, if she *had* been involved in an accident.

Apparently the constable agreed, because he said, 'Thanks for being so quick off the mark—the fire chaps say that it must have been touch and go that the engine didn't explode. They'll deal with it until it's no longer a danger and the guys can tow it away.' He looked at the silent woman.

'Elana, I'm sorry—it must be bringing back really bad memories. Right now, you need something hot to drink and someone to look after you. I'd take you home myself—'

'Phil, don't be silly,' she said weakly. Phil's wife was very pregnant. The last thing she'd need would be him arriving home with someone to look after.

His suspicions confirmed, Niko looked down at her white face. Without thinking, he took her arm and said firmly, 'She can stay at Mana. The homestead's not completely repaired yet, but it's liveable.'

He expected some resistance, and it was in a muted voice she said, 'No, that's not necessary. I'm fine.' But it took an obvious effort for her to stiffen her shoulders as she added, 'I just hope Jordan will be too.'

'The ambos think he's been lucky,' the constable reassured her. 'Not too much damage beyond a bad graze and possible cracked ribs. I hope so too, for his parents' sake. They'll be at the hospital to meet him.' He transferred his gaze to Niko. 'I don't think Elana should be driving. If you can drop her off at home I'll make sure her car gets back to her place.'

'Phil, it's not necessary.' Elana's tight voice made it obvious she didn't like being discussed as though she weren't there.

Niko intervened, 'You're mildly shocked. I'll take you home.'

She pulled away from him. 'I'm all right.' But her voice wavered on the final word.

'Be sensible.' He added crisply, 'Let the professionals take over.'

Her chin lifted. 'You're a professional?'

'No, but this man is. Come on, give him your keys.'

The cop was hiding a smile, one that almost escaped him when Elana stared indignantly at Niko for a few seconds, then shrugged. 'The keys are still in my car,' she said bleakly. 'OK, Phil, I won't drive if you think I shouldn't. I'll just collect my bag.'

Niko found himself admiring both her spirit and her common sense. He said, 'I could do with something hot and soothing right now. I'm pretty good at making coffee, but I'm thinking a tot of whisky should go into it.'

The lights of the remaining vehicles revealed both her disbelieving expression and a swift, narrowed glance. 'I hate whisky.'

Amused by her intransigence, Niko watched her head for her vehicle, and found himself wondering what had given her that sturdy spirit.

Once she was out of earshot the cop turned to him. 'Rotten thing to happen to her,' he said, frowning.

'To anyone,' Niko returned. Especially to the kid behind the wheel...

The young policeman went on, 'But tougher on Elana than most.' He hesitated, watching her as she opened her car door and bent inside it. 'She lost her parents—well, her stepfather—a couple of years or so ago in an accident. He was killed instantly, and her mother was so badly hurt she never walked again.'

Niko said harshly, 'Damn.'

'Yes. Elana was with them—they were hit head-on by an out-of-control truck.' He paused and shook his head. 'She was lucky—not too much in the way of injuries, but she had to leave a good job in Auckland to come home and look after Mrs Simmons—her mother. She died after a stroke about six months ago.' He paused. 'Hell of a shame for Elana to come across young Jordan like that.'

Niko looked towards her car. Elana was still

groping around in the front seat, presumably searching the bag she'd carried—a little satin thing that didn't look big enough to hold the keys to any house. Frowning, he watched her straighten up and step back, bag in hand.

He turned to the constable and extended his hand. 'I'm Niko Radcliffe from Mana Station.'

'Yeah, I recognised you from the photos in the local newspaper.'

They shook hands and turned to watch Elana walk back, clutching her bag, her face drawn and taut.

Niko opened the passenger door of his car. When she hesitated he said, 'Get in.'

Lips parting, she gave him a dark look, but clearly thought better of whatever she'd been going to say and obeyed, after thanking Phil Whoever-He-Was.

'I'll go and have a word with the fire brigade,' Niko told her, and closed the car door on her.

Turning away so she couldn't hear, he said quietly to the cop, 'I'll also ring my housekeeper; she'll stay the night and will keep an eye on her.'

The constable nodded. 'Great. She shouldn't be on her own. I'll get in touch with you when I know young Jordan's condition.' He paused, and gave a brief smile. 'But watch out for fireworks. Elana's pretty independent.'

However, when Niko returned to his car after being reassured that the leaking petrol was no longer a danger, Elana Grange looked far from independent. Eyes closed, she was leaning back in the seat, and even in the semi-darkness he could see that the colour hadn't returned to her face, and that her hands were clenched on her bag as though reliving the impact of a crash. A pang of compassion shook him.

At the sound of the opening door Elana forced up her weighted eyelids and took a deep breath. 'Thanks,' she said, adding, 'I didn't realise just how—how affected I'd be by this.'

'Accidents are always difficult to deal with, and for you now, I imagine much more so.'

So Phil had told him. She blinked back shaken tears. 'I thought—hoped—I'd got over it. The shock, I mean.'

Only to fall to pieces… Sometimes she wondered if she'd ever recover from the tragedy of her parents' deaths.

'Give it time,' Niko said as he set the car in motion. 'It's a truism, but time does heal most things—eventually.' He paused before adding, 'And if it doesn't entirely heal, it usually provides the ability to cope.'

Surprised, she looked up. His angular sculpted profile and the tone of his voice made her wonder if he'd discovered this for himself. Immediately she chided herself for her self-absorption. She wasn't the only person in the world to be forced to live with unexpected tragedy. Other people had even worse events in their lives, and managed to overcome their impact.

In a small voice she said, 'I just miss them so much.'

To her astonishment he dropped one hand from the wheel and closed it over hers. Although strong, his grip was warm and strangely comforting.

'That's the worst part,' he told her, releasing her cold fingers. 'But eventually you'll learn to live without them. And to be happy again.'

His pragmatic sympathy warmed some part of her that had been frozen so long she'd come to take it for granted. Had he too suffered a loss? Possibly. However, she wasn't comfortable discussing her grief with a man she didn't know, even though the events of the evening somehow seemed to form a link between them.

Opening her eyes, she gazed ahead as the head-lights revealed paddocks and fences and the sweep of a bay.

'Hey!' she exclaimed. 'Stop!'

'Why?' He kept on driving towards Mana homestead.

'You've gone past my gate. Sorry—I should have told you where I—'

'I know where you live.'

After digesting that she fought back bewilder-ment to demand, 'Then why did you drive past?'

'Because I agree with your policeman friend. You shouldn't be on your own tonight.'

Silenced by a mixture of shock and outrage, she opened her mouth to speak, only to have her throat close and the words refuse to emerge.

The man beside her went on, 'I called my house-keeper and she's preparing a bed for you.' And without pausing he added on an ironic note, 'I'm sure there will be a lock on the door. If not, you'll still be quite safe.'

Stung, she blurted, 'I didn't—I wasn't...'

Housekeeper? Did he travel with a domestic ménage? Although various tradesmen and deco-rators had been working on the sadly neglected and almost derelict Mana homestead for some months, local gossip hadn't mentioned a resident housekeeper.

Perhaps Niko Radcliffe guessed her thoughts, because he said calmly, 'I assume you know that the house is still being restored, although fortunately it's almost finished.'

Elana drew in a sharp breath. 'It's been the talk of the district since you bought the station.' Along with the huge amount of money he was spending on the house as well as the land itself. 'But I'm perfectly all right—a bit shaken, that's all. I don't need to be cosseted.'

'Your policeman friend didn't seem to think so.'

His amused tone rubbed her raw. 'Phil's a nice man but he's always had an over-developed protective instinct. There's no need for you to wake up your housekeeper and put her to this trouble.'

'She's another with an over-developed protective instinct,' he said laconically, turning the wheel to swing between low stone walls. For years they'd proudly guarded the entrance to Mana homestead, but now more than a few of the volcanic boulders had tumbled to the ground.

No doubt they'd soon be put back in place.

Above the clatter of the cattle stop, Elana said grittily, 'I—thank you.' In his forceful, domineering way, Niko Radcliffe possibly thought he was being neighbourly.

'It's nothing.'

His tone told her that, indeed, he meant just that. Because, of course, his housekeeper would be the one who did any actual caring—not that it would be necessary.

She opened her mouth to say something astringent, then closed it as he went on, 'It's been an unnerving experience for you—and understandably so.'

'Which doesn't mean I'm not capable of looking after myself.'

'Is it always so difficult for you to accept help?'

Elana couldn't come up with any sensible response. Much as she resisted the idea, her shock at the accident and fear for Jordan weren't the only reasons for her silence. From the moment she'd seen Niko he'd had a potent effect on her.

And she certainly wasn't going to let him know that.

He broke the silence. 'If Mrs Nixon had been with us, I'm sure you'd have let her sweep you off home with her.'

'I—' Elana paused, then said reluctantly, 'Well—

yes. But I've known the Nixons almost all my life, and she'd worry.'

Still amused, he said, 'I can't say I'd *worry*, but I'd certainly be concerned if I'd dropped you off by yourself. And if you're concerned now about local gossip, you don't have to be. My house-keeper will be enough of a chaperone.'

His response made her seem like some virgin from Victorian melodrama. Elana stifled a sharp retort. 'I'm not at all worried about my—well, about my safety. Or my reputation. I just want to go home.'

'No,' he said coolly.

Fulminating, she looked across at a profile hewn of stone, all arrogant angles above a chin that proclaimed complete determination.

Sheer frustration made her demand recklessly, 'Why are you doing this? You realise that it's kidnapping?'

His mouth curved. 'Tell me, would anyone in Waipuna accept that—and I'm including your policeman friend?'

He'd called her bluff. Of course they wouldn't, and neither would she accuse him of it. Curtly she retorted, 'I'd have preferred that we talk the matter over before you drove past my gate.'

'Why? We'd have just had exactly the same conversation, only sooner. And I'm assuming that you're sensible enough to accept that you're not only tired, but still traumatised by the tragedy of your parents' accident.'

Elana flinched, averting her face as he stopped the car outside the old homestead. The harsh glare of the headlights highlighted the amazing change huge amounts of money could produce in a few months. Evidence of years of neglect under the previous owner had been erased, and Mana homestead looked as pristine as it must have when it had first been built over a century ago.

Niko turned and inspected her. She was staring at the homestead, her features sharpened. 'I've upset you. I'm sorry,' he said, resisting the impulse to take her hands in his and offer what comfort he could.

Years ago he'd learned a harsh lesson about giving in to a compassionate impulse. A friend's daughter had suffered a setback, and he'd taken her on a short cruise on his yacht, only to realise that she was falling in love with him. He'd felt no more for her than a brotherly affection, and had told her so as gently as he could. For the rest of his life, he'd be grateful that her attempt at suicide had failed, and that she was now happily married.

Since then, he'd been careful not to raise expectations he wasn't able to satisfy, choosing sophisticated lovers who understood that he wasn't interested in matrimony.

Elana Grange shook her head, her tone flat when she answered. 'I'm rather weary of telling people I'm all right. Thank you. You're being very kind.' She even attempted a smile as she straightened her shoulders and said in what she probably hoped was her normal voice, 'It's shocking what twenty years of neglect did to this place. Those pohutukawa trees on the edge of the beach are over three hundred years old. The previous owners were going to cut them down. They said they blocked the view.'

'Why didn't they fell them?'

'There was a public outcry, and a threat to take it to the environment court. I don't know why they wanted them removed. They almost never came to Mana.' She paused. 'And the oak tree we've just passed was planted by the wife of the very first settler here.'

'I gather from your tone that you're not sure whether or not I'm going to bulldoze trees down,' Niko said dryly.

Elana hesitated, before telling him the truth. 'It hadn't occurred to me, but I hope you're not.'

'I prefer to plant trees rather than kill them.'

Brief and to the point, and, because he'd decided to restore the homestead rather than demolish it, she believed him. 'Except for pine trees, I believe.'

'Except for wilding pines,' he agreed.

He switched off the engine and got out. On a ragged, deep breath, Elana fumbled with the clip of her seatbelt, then wrestled with the unfamiliar door catch. Before she'd fathomed it out, the door swung open.

'Here, take my hand,' Niko commanded.

Scrambling out, she muttered, 'Thanks, but I'm fine.'

Although he said nothing, she realised he was watching her closely as they walked towards the house. A woman opened the door—the housekeeper, of course—probably in her forties, with a smile that held both a welcome and some interest.

Niko said, 'Elana, this is Mrs West. Patty, Elana Grange lives next door. She's had a shock, so I'd suggest a cup of tea or coffee.' He glanced down at Elana. 'Or something a bit stronger.'

'Tea will be fine, thank you,' Elana said as crisply as she could, and added, 'I'm sorry Mr Radcliffe felt obliged to put you to all this trouble.'

The older woman's smile widened. 'It's no trouble. I've made you up a bed in a room overlooking the beach.'

'Thank you.' Although it had to be very late Elana was no longer tired. Just strung on wires. Tea might help her to think clearly.

Why on earth had she surrendered to Niko's calm abduction?

The answer stared her in the face. Jordan's accident had flung her back into the shock of losing Steve and, later, her mother.

It was too late now to regret her weakness. She was here at Mana, and, thanks to both Phil and Niko Radcliffe's over-developed sense of responsibility, she had no way of getting home.

Five minutes later she was sitting on a comfortable sofa in a room that breathed sophisticated country style, fighting an aching weariness that clouded her mind. Barely able to prop her eyelids up, she covered a prodigious yawn.

Sitting down had not been a good move. Right then she desired nothing more than the blessed oblivion of sleep—in her own bed. Her eyes were full of grit, and somehow her bones had crumbled. The thought of getting to her feet made her want to curl up and collapse, crash out on the sofa for what was left of the night.

Niko's black brows drew together. 'You're exhausted. Do you want to forego the tea?'

'No.' Her voice sounded oddly distant. She set her shoulders and tried for a smile, failing dismally.

'You did well,' he told her, his voice level.

'So did you.'

Always, until she died, she'd remember how he looked as he dragged Jordan free of the car, the sheer brute strength of the man, and the fierce determination in his face as he carried the youth to safety.

Taking a deep breath, she said, 'I'm going to take the next first-aid course the St John's people advertise.'

'An excellent idea, although I hope you never have to deal with a situation like that again.'

The urgent summons of a cell phone startled her. A mixture of adrenalin and concern forced her shakily upwards.

After a moment she realised Niko was holding out a hand to her. A cold fist of dread closing around her heart, she staggered to her feet. His fingers closed around hers, summoning a tingle of primal awareness that sizzled through her, giving her enough energy to stay upright.

He flicked his phone open, was silent a second or two, then said crisply, 'Speaking. How is he?'

CHAPTER THREE

SWALLOWING, ELANA PREPARED herself for bad news.

Time stretched unbearably in the silence before Niko Radcliffe said in a vastly different tone, 'He's regained consciousness? Great. And at his age bruised or cracked ribs should heal quickly. It doesn't sound as though his other injuries will be any problem. He was lucky.'

Elana sagged, grateful for the strength of his arm around her. Despising herself for her weakness, she tried to pull away, only to find she couldn't.

'Yes, I'll make sure she knows,' he finished. 'Thanks very much.'

And released her after he'd snapped the cell phone shut and tossed it onto the nearest chair. 'That was your policeman friend. The ambulance people seem pretty convinced that young Jordan has nothing more than mild concussion, a shallow cut from flying glass, and what will probably be quite severe bruises caused by the seatbelt, but just might be cracked ribs.'

The mixture of relief and her body's fierce, involuntary response to his nearness set Elana's pulses hammering. Startled, she tried to pull back.

'Sit down,' Niko ordered, eyes narrowing as he scanned her face. 'You're just about out on your feet.' He released her, frowning as she sat too quickly onto the sofa. 'You need something stronger than tea.'

She stiffened her backbone, resisting another debilitating wave of tiredness. 'I don't normally go to pieces. Thank heavens Jordan got off so lightly. I'm very glad he was wearing his seatbelt.'

'Only an idiot would drive without one.' His voice was coolly dismissive.

That tone—so dispassionate as to border on contempt—summoned harsh, painful memories of her father. Catapulted back to childhood, she looked up into her host's hard face, then glanced away.

He went on curtly, 'Especially a kid who doesn't know how to drive safely on a back-country road.'

Mrs West came in carrying a tray, and frowned

as she set the tray down on a table. 'Goodness, Ms Grange, you're as white as a ghost. I think you could do with some brandy in that tea.'

Bracing herself, Elana managed a smile. 'No, really, the tea will work wonders. Actually, I'm reacting to *good* news.'

And a chilling flashback...

'Young Jordan was very lucky,' Niko explained, and briefly told the housekeeper the extent of Jordan's injuries.

'Oh, that's wonderful!' Mrs West gave a wry smile. 'Well, you know what I mean! Better bruised ribs than a broken back.'

As she left the room her employer moved across to the tray and asked Elana how she drank tea.

'As is,' she said, 'no milk, no sugar.'

Niko poured a cup of tea and brought it across to her. Gratefully lifting it, Elana began to sip, using the action as a kind of shield against that intimidating ice-blue gaze.

Pull yourself together, she told herself. *Stop being so feeble!* To fill the silence she said, 'This has not been the most auspicious introduction to Waipuna for you. I hope any other visits will be much less dramatic.'

'I hope so too, as I plan to visit frequently.' At her surprised glance he added crisply, 'At least until Mana Station is up and running again the way it should be.'

It would do no harm to spread the word that he intended to take a personal interest in the station. He was no micro-manager, and he trusted Dave West, the new manager, but he intended to make the important decisions for the station's future.

And, he thought grimly, make sure they were carried out.

It should have been a pleasant extra that Elana Grange lived right next door. Even now, in spite of dark circles beneath her eyes and features sharpened by tiredness, her subtle magnetism stirred his blood. But independent though she clearly was, it was unlikely she'd be sophisticated enough to understand the sort of relationships he preferred.

So he wouldn't be giving in to that primal summons.

'Why the startled look?' he enquired.

'I suppose—well, I thought you'd be an absentee owner,' she admitted. 'Your life must keep you busy.'

He shrugged. 'For most of their history the people of San Mari had to produce all their own food or starve. Sometimes they starved. So tending their cattle and the land that supported them was hugely important. Things have changed now with the advent of communications and tourism, of course. However, vast areas of the world still need food, and along with my other responsibilities I do what I can to supply it.'

Responsibilities? Elana allowed herself a small smile. That was an interesting way to describe the worldwide empire he'd built for himself. And although he might consider himself a farmer, very few men of the land wielded so much influence and power.

His brows lifted. 'I said something amusing?'

'No.' She hesitated, met his narrowed gaze and expanded, 'I made the mistake of assuming you'd be more like the previous owners, who used Mana as a cash cow so they could live the life they enjoyed.'

His expression warned her he didn't like what she'd said. 'Stereotyping is lazy thinking,' he told her coolly.

'True,' she admitted, and sipped more tea, welcoming its comfort and reassurance as a wave of intense weariness washed over her.

Her host asked, 'Is there anything else besides that tea that you need?'

'Thanks, but it's done the trick. You were right—I'm already feeling better.' She smothered a yawn with a hand. 'I'm sorry, I think it's time I went to bed.'

'Patty will be back in a minute or so to show you your room,' he said. 'If you need anything, ask her.'

Sure enough, the housekeeper appeared almost immediately, and, after saying goodnight and being ordered to sleep well, Elana was ushered up the stairs into a bedroom that breathed luxury without being fussy or ostentatious.

When she didn't have to force her eyelids to stay up, Elana knew she'd appreciate it even more.

Mrs West offered her a nightgown, saying with a smile, 'It's mine, so it won't fit you, but it'll cover you.'

Exhaustion weighed Elana down, slowed her brain, dragged through every word. 'That's very kind of you.'

Drat Niko Radcliffe. Why couldn't he have delivered her home?

Her expression must have revealed her thoughts, because Mrs West said, 'The *en suite* for this room isn't functional yet, but there's a bathroom two doors down the hall to the left. I've put toothpaste and some towels there for you.'

Elana thanked her and set off. It took all the concentration she could muster to wash her face and clean her teeth.

Back in the bedroom Mrs West said as she left, 'The light in the hall will be on, so if you need to go to the bathroom later you'll have no trouble finding your way here. Goodnight and sleep well.'

Feeling as though she'd been beaten with cudgels, Elana climbed into a nightgown several sizes too big, and sank into the enormous bed, gratefully allowing unconsciousness to claim her.

But with sleep came dreams—the same nightmares that had tortured her after the accident. Unable to prevent them, she relived again the horror of seeing the huge stock truck hurtle towards them, her mother's scream cut off by the moment of impact, the pain mercifully shortened by a devouring darkness.

And then thank all the gods, she woke up, whimpering, and stumbled up to her feet, her heart thudding so strongly she felt it might jump out of her breast. After switching on the lamp on the bedside table, she drew in several deep breaths before realising she needed to head for the bathroom.

'Two doors down,' she muttered, clutching the over-large gown around her. 'On the left...'

The hall light was dim, but she could see easily enough to make out the bathroom door. Tiptoeing, she got there, and was halfway back to her bedroom when she heard a noise behind her. Heart jumping, she increased her pace and prayed for it to be the housekeeper.

'Elana.'

No such luck. The deep hard voice belonged to Niko Radcliffe. Hand groping to pull the wide neck of the nightdress up, she swivelled around. He loomed in the semi-darkness, big and tall and far too close, and showing far too much skin.

At first she thought he was naked and took a short step backwards as her stunned gaze took in wide, tanned shoulders and a muscled chest with a scroll of dark hair across it. A swift relief eased some of her shock when she realised he was wearing pyjama trousers.

'What...?' she breathed.

He took two strides towards her, stopping as

she backed away. Frowning, he asked, 'Are you properly awake?'

She ran her tongue over dry lips. 'Of course I am,' she said huskily. 'I needed to use the bathroom.'

'You're shaking. I hope you're not afraid of me.'

Something in his tone made her stiffen. 'No, of course not.' Despairingly, she realised her voice was thin and almost wavering. She had to steady it to continue, 'I'm all right. I—I'm—'

She stopped and shook her head, dragging in more air in a quick gasp. 'Sorry,' she whispered.

He waited a few seconds before saying in a milder tone, 'Can you walk?'

'Yes.'

But when she took a step her legs crumpled beneath her. Mortified, she leant against the wall and clamped her eyes shut to stop the walls—and her host—from suddenly spinning.

'I'll carry you,' he said harshly, and before she could protest she was enveloped in his warmth and strength, the faint, potent male scent of him somehow comforting as well as stimulating, so that she had to fight a craving to rest her head on his shoulder.

'I'm too heavy,' she managed as he lifted her.

'You're not. Just keep still and I'll get you back to your bed.'

Wordlessly, her thoughts and emotions a tangled jumble, she obeyed.

When he straightened after lowering her into the bed she shivered again, suddenly cold and bereft. The light of the lamp picked out the strong bone structure of Niko's face, and a sudden, unexpected sensation gripped her, a kind of urgency, of hunger...

Something in the Count's gaze made her realise that the nightdress neckline had dragged down, revealing far too much of her breasts. Scarlet-faced, she hauled the material up, grateful that he'd immediately turned to pull the duvet over her.

Stone-faced, he said, 'I'll get you something to drink.'

'Not whisky,' she managed with a weak smile.

His answering smile heated every cell in her body. 'No, not whisky.'

She watched him stride from the room, his lithe strength quickening her pulse rate. Body tight with a dangerous tension, she dragged in a deep, shuddering breath and hauled herself up against the pillows, pulling up the duvet to cover her breasts.

How stupid—how *idiotic*—to practically faint, like some Victorian debutante confronted by a man in night attire...

Niko returned almost immediately, a glass of water in his hand. Elana was lying back against the pillows, her hair falling in a cloud of rose-gold silk across her shoulders. He dragged in a sharp breath at the memory of ivory breasts cupped by fabric that hugged every curve, of a faint, elusive perfume, of the feel of her warm body against his.

She tantalised every sense. All compassion momentarily swamped by a dangerous hunger, Niko stiffened. Then he noticed the tears glittering beneath her lashes. She was in no fit state for anything other than sexless comfort.

'Here,' he said, hoping she wasn't aware of the rough note beneath the words, 'drink this.'

Elana reached out, only to have the duvet fall down. Colour staining her skin, she grabbed the material and hauled it up to her shoulders.

Niko put the glass of water—flavoured by about a teaspoonful of brandy—into her hand. It was still shaking, he noted. Controlling his expression, he said austerely, 'This is why your police-man friend was convinced you shouldn't be alone tonight.'

She stiffened. Alone, she'd have dealt with the aftermath of her nightmare. She wouldn't be fighting this—this weird response.

Hastily she lowered her face and began to drink, praying the heat and colour would fade from her face and shoulders. The liquid caught her breath, but she gulped it down, intent on banishing the aftermath of her nightmare.

Go away, she commanded silently. *Leave me alone, for heaven's sake.*

But the Radcliffe man stayed until the last drop was drained.

'Thank you.' She prayed he couldn't realise how much effort it took to control her voice. 'You've been very kind. I'm OK now.'

'Do you want me to sit with you until you get back to sleep? Or get Patty West to stay with you until then?'

She shook her head so vigorously she had to push back a swathe of damp hair from her face. Surely he had to be joking! Besides, it was sleep that summoned the nightmare, not wakefulness. 'I'll be fine,' she repeated.

Eyes hooded, he looked down at her and nodded. 'All right. I'll see you in the morning.'

Once the door closed behind him Elana tried to relax, to breathe slowly and loosen every tense muscle.

Nothing worked; every sinew, every nerve in her body remained taut, and snatches of thought whirled chaotically around her brain. A glance at her watch told her she'd only had a couple of hours' sleep, not nearly long enough to sate the voracious tiredness that had gripped her. Yet it had gone, replaced by a sharp burst of energy.

Once again she lay back against the pillow, closed her eyes and tried to concentrate on easing tension, calling on the defence mechanisms she'd developed when she'd been a child trying to block out the sound of her mother weeping.

But disturbing memories forced their way through—not childhood pain nor the phantoms of the nightmare, but that moment when her host had looked down at her in the bed and hunger had flared in his arctic eyes.

Alarmed, she'd had to force herself to resist an answering need, something much stronger than awareness and infinitely more potent than normal feminine admiration for a good-looking man. Niko Radcliffe was much more than handsome; he projected a compelling masculinity that both unsettled and excited her.

Her father had been just such a man. Yet his smooth sophistication had been a cover for violence.

Three years ago she'd fallen in love, only to discover that she was following a familiar pattern. Behind her closed lids she saw her mother's face, heard her mother's voice when she'd consoled her daughter after that bitter break-up.

'I'm so glad you had the courage to walk out on Roland,' she'd said quietly. 'I was a coward. It took far too long for me to understand what your father was doing to me—and to you. I was the happiest girl in the world when I married him. I believed he loved me, and I was sure I loved him.' Tears had sprung into her eyes. 'But what he felt for me wasn't love, it was possessiveness, a driving need to control.' She hesitated, then said, 'And when he used force to gain that control, he felt it was my fault, not his, that he hit me.'

Elana remembered admitting bleakly, 'I've always vowed I'd never make the same mistake.

And at least Roland didn't beat me. But how can
you tell the difference between love and possessiveness early enough—early enough to be able
to get away before it's too late? Before you fall
in love.'

Her mother's face twisted. 'Oh, darling, if I
could give you a set of rules I would. I can't. But
after I left your father and found Steve, I realised
that what I'd believed to be love was actually desire. I'd been flattered that your father wanted me,
even though he and I had nothing in common.'

Elana turned her head on the pillow and closed
her eyes.

Her mother's words were etched on her brain
cells. 'Desire on its own isn't enough. You need
to be friends too. When you fall for a man who
excites you, if you can't think of him as a friend
it's not love. It's just lust, and it's dangerous.'

For her second marriage her mother had chosen her very best friend, and they had all been so
happy together...

Steve hadn't been perfect. A cheerful, slapdash
man, he'd made no secret of his adoration for her
mother, and he'd met Elana's childish suspicion
with tenderness and understanding until she too
had learned to love him, to feel safe with him.

She blinked and opened her eyes, staring across the elegant room. Moonlight seeped through a narrow crack in the curtains, and through the glass she could hear the soft hush of waves, the sound that sent her to sleep at home.

Her mother had been wrong when she'd said she couldn't give her a set of rules.

...a man you can't call a friend...

Niko Radcliffe was dangerous. She couldn't imagine him being a mere friend to any woman.

Her wildfire, tantalising response to him wasn't—and never would be—anything more than a strong sexual reaction.

Forewarned, she thought sardonically, *is fore-armed. A good mantra to keep you safe...*

A soft knock on the door woke her. She blinked at the sunlight through the drapes across the window, and for a second wondered where she was.

'Elana? Can I come in?' Mrs West asked.

'Yes, of course.'

The door opened. 'I thought I'd better wake you now, or you wouldn't be able to get to sleep at all tonight,' the housekeeper said as she approached the bed, a plastic bag dangling from her hand.

'What time is it?'

'Eleven o'clock.'

Dismayed, Elana blinked at her. 'Heavens,' she said faintly. 'I've never slept so late in all my life before. Thank you very much.'

'You clearly needed the rest.' Mrs West gave a cautious smile. 'I'm afraid I broke into your house. The boss suggested it, so I sneaked in here this morning and took your key from your bag, then drove to your place and collected a change of clothes for you. I hope you don't mind.'

She held out the bag and the key.

After a startled moment Elana replied with real gratitude, 'Not at all. Thank you so much.'

'The boss thought it would be better if I did it rather than him. And I was sure you'd feel a lot better in clean clothing. He's out on the farm right now, but he said to tell you he'll drive you home whenever you want to go.'

'Thank you,' Elana said again, and added, 'I'm sorry he dragged you away from home last night to look after me.'

Mrs West shook her head vigorously. 'Oh, he's a good boss—tough but very fair. My husband and I, we feel very lucky to be here.'

Half an hour later, showered and refreshed and in clean clothes, Elana made her way into the parlour and sat down a little limply in a large arm-chair. Mrs West had chosen well; a pair of jeans and a T-shirt with clean undergarments gave her strength.

Until the sound of an approaching vehicle set her nerves jangling again.

Stiffening her spine, she scrambled up and walked across to the window to look over what had once been a lawn to the beach. Although the house had been almost fully restored to beauty, the garden scrambled down to the beach, wildly unkempt, a jungle of neglected bushes and trees and a roughly mown lawn. The tide was in, and the sun had turned the estuary into a molten sheet of gold. In summer, just in time for the Christmas holidays, the ancient pohutukawa trees marking the boundary between land and sea would set the water on fire with the threadlike bounty of their dropped flowers.

Normally the view would have lifted her heart. But when she heard her name from behind she jumped and whirled around, a hand pressed to her chest.

'What the hell—?' Niko Radcliffe demanded harshly, taking two long strides to grip her shoulders and hold her upright as her knees struggled to support her.

'I'm all right,' she said, the words jumbled together. She swallowed. 'You can let me go.'

He scanned her face with clinical detachment, before releasing her and stepping back, his gaze narrowed and intent.

After a deep breath she stumbled into speech. 'Sorry, I didn't realise you were so—so nearby. I heard the quad bike but it seemed quite a distance away.'

He shrugged. 'I wasn't on it.'

Another sharp breath gave her the strength to say, 'I'm not normally so neurotic.' She braced herself. 'Thank you for everything you've done— including the idea of collecting some clothes for me.'

His brows rose. 'You surprise me.'

'Why?' she asked, startled.

'I suspected you'd be annoyed at the invasion of your privacy.'

'Not a bit.' He was still standing too close, and those hard eyes were too inquisitorial. Why didn't he back off? Squaring her shoulders, she asked, 'Have you heard anything about Jordan this morning?'

'Yes. He's recovering well, and sent his thanks to us. So did his parents. They were worried about your reaction to the accident.'

'You didn't—'

He read her mind. 'I told them the truth, that you were sound asleep.'

Elana let out a swift breath. 'Thanks. They're nice people and they have enough to worry about right now.' She looked up at him and managed to produce a smile. 'You've been very kind, but if it's not too inconvenient I'd like to go home.'

'Mrs West is making lunch for us.'

'Oh,' she said inadequately.

'You must be hungry.'

As though in answer her stomach rumbled softly. She produced a wry smile, and looked up to meet one that almost rocked her back on her heels.

'Clearly I am,' she admitted, her voice a little rough.

Niko's smile was *something*—a mixture of understanding and genuine amusement that sent a shiver of excitement through every cell in her body. She had a sudden, terrifying insight into her mother's inability to resist her father.

Her thoughts were interrupted as her host said, 'Then come and eat.'

His intonation reminded her that although he'd been born in New Zealand he'd spent much of his life in Europe. And the way he offered his arm emphasised that heritage. Elana placed her hand on it, awareness sizzling through her at the hard flexion of the muscles beneath her fingers as they walked side by side down the hall.

He was no effete aristocrat, this man. Into her mind flashed a memory of him carrying Jordan away from the car, and she shivered.

'What is it?' he demanded.

'I was thinking about last night—what might have happened if Jordan's car had caught fire. I'm so grateful it didn't.'

'Indeed,' he said decisively.

'I hope Jordan's learnt something from it.'

'Especially not to take corners too fast on narrow gravel roads,' Niko returned, his tone verging on unsympathetic. 'You said he's around eighteen years old?'

Elana nodded. 'About that. Certainly not much older.' After a silent moment she added, 'But old enough to know better.'

'A dangerous age—you tend to believe you're bulletproof.'

She said quietly, 'Yes.' Yet somehow she found it impossible to picture the man beside her flaunting the careless, dangerous arrogance of youth. He was too controlled, so formidably self-contained it was impossible to tell what he was thinking.

Mrs West had set the meal out on a terrace overlooking the beach, the beams overhead festooned in foliage from a vigorous creeper that allowed golden sunlight in shifting patterns on the tiles.

'Oh.' Elana stopped and stared around. 'Oh, this is lovely!'

'Apart from the surroundings,' her host said dryly and pulled a chair out for her. 'I'm looking for a good landscape architect. Do you happen to know of one?'

'I'm sorry, I don't.' Elana sat down. 'Certainly not in Waipuna.'

Niko sent her an ironic glance as he walked around to the other side of the table. 'I didn't think there'd be one here.' He sat down, and in the same tone said, 'You must have been a charming baby with that amazing hair.'

Startled—both by the abrupt change of subject and the sensation sizzling down her spine and heating her cheekbones—Elana was suddenly intensely aware of his lithe economy of movement, of the strength in those broad shoulders.

Searching for a light response, she managed, 'Apparently it's an inheritance from my grandmother, although it skipped a generation. My mother was a true blonde.'

'Genetics are an interesting study.' He glanced around the wild tangle of foliage that bordered the overgrown lawn. 'I've been told this was once a superb garden.'

'It used to be beautiful.' She added, 'But even now it has a wild beauty.'

He nodded. 'It reminds me of a book I had as a child—a book of fairy tales. It had a picture of the garden around Sleeping Beauty's castle. For some reason it intrigued me.'

Elana looked up, met quizzical blue eyes, and experienced another disturbing jolt of electricity. Hoping her voice was steady, she replied, 'Perhaps we had the same book. Mine had flowering vines—blackberry vines, I suspect, judging by the thorns—tangled around a tower.'

Niko asked, 'Do you think that might have had some influence on your decision to work in a florist shop?'

'No.' She'd taken the part-time job because it was the only one available in Waipuna at the time, and she needed the money. Shrugging, she finished, 'Although, who knows? Like genetics, the unconscious works in interesting ways.'

Half an hour later she set down an empty cup of strong black coffee and looked across the table. Her stomach clenched in unnerving anticipation as a ray of sunlight caught Niko's face, outlining his features in gold. Deep inside her, something wild and uncontrollable coalesced into heat and fire.

She had to draw breath to say, 'Thank you, that was just what I needed. I'll thank Mrs West and then I need to go home.'

He got up. 'Of course,' he said calmly. 'I'll take you.'

Clearly she had no choice in the matter. Nevertheless, she tried. 'Thank you, but it's not necessary. Mrs West brought me a pair of flat shoes as well as my clothes, so I'll walk home. It's only a kilometre away.'

And received another ironic smile. 'I'm sure you could walk it, but my mother would be horrified if I let you.'

A little bewildered, she sent him a disbelieving look. 'She'd never know.'

His shoulders lifted in a shrug. 'I'd know.' His tone confirming that she had no option.

Elana fumed in silent frustration. Some women might find a dominant male an intriguing challenge, but there was a difference between dominant and domineering. Bristling, she realised that Niko Radcliffe came too close to being domineering.

Like her father. And Roland...

Not that it mattered. Once she got home she'd probably never see Niko again. 'Thank you,' she repeated sedately.

Five minutes later, after thanking his housekeeper for her help, she was ensconced in his large car, her discarded clothes from the previous night neatly packed in a plastic bag.

Niko glanced sideways, noting that most of the colour had come back into her ivory skin. Apart from looking a little tired she seemed in good shape. Deliberately keeping the conversation impersonal, he soon had her chatting about the district, enjoying her dry wit as she told him about some of the families who lived and farmed along the peninsula.

As they approached the entrance to Mana he asked, 'Are you descended from one of the pioneering families here?'

'Far from it—we first came here on holiday and stayed in a friend's bach.' She smiled. 'A little holiday shack. I believe you South Islanders call them cribs.'

'I believe they do,' he said, amused. 'I've never considered myself to be a South Islander. Or a New Zealander, come to that.'

She sent him a startled look, then nodded. 'That's understandable. But with dual citizenship you have two countries to call home.'

Surprised, Niko realised he called no place home. Although his mother had taken him back to her father's palace, the huge, echoing building with its gilt and crimson furniture had been no home to him. And the boarding school and universities he'd attended had been the same. His grandfather and his uncle, the next Prince of San Mari, had always been busy with affairs of state.

And although he'd enjoyed them, the holidays spent in the old stone house on the steep, tussock slopes of his father's merino sheep station had never been long enough to put down roots.

Perhaps that was why he'd bought Mana Station. For a home base?

He dismissed the idea. 'So your parents fell in love with the area,' he prompted.

A beam of sunlight fired her hair into an aureole as she nodded. 'Exactly. They liked it so much Steve—my stepfather—got a job in Waipuna, and they bought the bach. It was just a bunkhouse then, with a primitive kitchen and an outdoor shower. Steve and my mother turned it into a proper home.'

Alerted by a note of reserve in her words, Niko glanced at her again. Her full mouth was held in a straight line, as though talking of the past pained her.

Or made her angry. Had her mother and father divorced?

Hell, he understood how she might feel; the dissolution of a marriage, whether by divorce or death, was hugely bewildering for children. He could just remember his own confusion and anguish when his mother had taken him to San Mari. He'd missed his father immensely. And still regretted that he'd never been able to forge a proper relationship with him before he'd died.

Beside him, Elana said quietly, 'It's the next gate on the left. You can let me off there—it's not very far to the house.'

'I'll take you all the way,' he said calmly.

About a hundred metres down a narrow drive between the slender grey trunks of more kanuka trees, the house and a separate garage appeared. As they drew to a stop Niko realised the house must have been barely larger than a garden shed before Elana's stepfather added to it.

The buildings snuggled into a flowery garden that stretched towards a low bluff. Sprawling pohutukawa trees formed a green edging to the little cove he knew to be Anchor Bay, its amber curve facing a wide stretch of glittering, island-dotted water. On the far side of the estuary a range of rolling green hills met the sky.

As he got out of the car, Niko looked around. Casual, a little untidy, the garden was humming with bees and bright with flowers. A monarch butterfly flitted through a tangle of low shrubs, brightly orange against green leaves.

Rounding the back of the vehicle, he got an excellent view of Elana's long, elegant legs as she climbed out. A swift, savage hunger bit into him, speeding his heart rate, sending an instant message to every cell in his body.

Damn, *damn*, he thought, angered by his lack of control. He hadn't had such a fierce, predatory response like this since adolescence...

He bent to close the door behind her while she took a few steps towards the house. When he straightened she turned to face him and held out her hand.

Gold-flecked green gaze meeting his directly, her skin stained slightly pink, she said in a level stiff voice, 'Thank you very much for your help and support.'

Very formal, he thought sardonically.

'It was little enough,' he said as they shook hands, and added, 'Patty West did any looking after that was necessary. I hope the accident hasn't affected you too much.'

Her gaze didn't waver, but he thought some of the colour faded from her skin. A kind of regret made him moderate his tone. 'If you need anything, let me know.'

'Thank you,' she said politely, her tone making it clear she had no intention of doing any such thing.

For some futile and unnecessary reason her unspoken refusal exasperated him as much as the cool smile she bestowed on him before turning away to walk towards the house.

Niko waited until she'd unlocked the front door and swivelled around to lift her hand in farewell, before inclining his head, getting back into the car and starting the engine.

He put off any speculation about his unexpected, disturbing reaction to her until he reached Mana Station. Once there, instead of going into the homestead he walked over the untended lawn, stopping at the top of the low bank that bordered the beach. Elana Grange was exactly the sort of woman he'd vowed never to become involved with again—young and unsophisticated.

Frowning, he told himself he'd long since got past the stage of bedding—or wanting to bed— every woman he found sexy. Until he'd seen Elana at the ball he'd been coolly in control of his emotions.

This unwanted, reckless response to her had to be more of a chemical reaction than an emotional one, he decided wryly, one that both surprised and exasperated him. And it would pass.

While he was at Mana he'd be a good neighbour to Elana, and that was all.

Turning, he inspected the homestead. The original architect had combined elements of Georgian serenity with the lighter, more informal verandas and terraces of a tropical plantation home. However, over the years clumsy alterations had been made, cluttering the clean, simple lines.

According to the architect who'd surveyed it after he'd bought the station, it would take as much money and time to restore it to its original state as it would to knock it down completely and erect a new building in its place.

Common sense had told Niko to do just that. Although he planned to keep a close eye on Mana Station he wasn't planning to live there permanently, and even if he were, the last thing he needed was a big, old-fashioned mansion built for a Victorian family. A modern beach house would have been a sensible replacement.

Yet growing up in a palace over three hundred years old, in a country where tradition was an important part of life, meant he'd had the homestead restored and renovated.

Now to do the same to the garden.
Elana had described it as once beautiful.
Given time, it would be again.

CHAPTER FOUR

'HAVE YOU ANY idea of what Niko Radcliffe plans to do with Mana homestead now that it's as good as new?' Mrs Nixon asked.

Hiding a smile, Elana looked up from tying a ribbon around a posy. She'd been expecting this. Mrs Nixon couldn't be called an inveterate gossip, but she did like to know what was happening in the district.

Unfortunately for her, one night spent at Mana homestead a week ago didn't give Elana a hot line to the Radcliffe man's plans. 'No idea at all,' she said cheerfully.

'So it's just the way it used to look, like that old print in the library?'

"That old print" was a charming sketch reputed to be drawn by the first woman to live at Mana homestead. 'From what I remember, exactly the same,' Elana told her, ringing up the sale.

'Perhaps he's planning to sell it. Or turn it into a lodge?'

'I suppose that's a possibility,' Elana returned, suppressing an odd reluctance to speculate. She added, 'It would make a fabulous lodge.'

'It would, wouldn't it? And it's not as though he's likely to spend much time—if any—there.'

Elana handed over the posy she'd just assembled. 'Here you are.'

'Thank you, dear.' While Elana dealt with her credit card Mrs Nixon leaned forward. In a lowered voice, she said, 'I had a call from Margot Percy yesterday. Greg's not ready to retire yet but apparently all his years of managing Mana don't cut any ice when he applies for a position. Margot said he's getting depressed, saying that all the employers seemed to want someone young and active.'

Surprised, Elana said, 'Really? I know he resigned when Niko Radcliffe bought the place, but I assumed he must have had another place to go to.'

'I thought so too.' In an even lower voice Mrs Nixon confided, 'But Margot told me—and I know I don't have to ask you to keep this confidential—that the Count actually sacked Greg.'

Elana's mild curiosity turned into shock. '*Sacked* him? *Why?*'

'He doesn't know. Just a curt interview, apparently, then, *Pow!—you're sacked.*' She drew a deep breath. 'I really feel for them. Greg's in his late fifties now, and it doesn't look good for them at all.'

Elana felt sick. Somehow she'd allowed herself to be lulled into believing that Niko Radcliffe had a softer side, and some human feelings. 'Where are the Percys now?'

'Oh, they've got a rather nice bach over on the West Coast, quite near Dargaville, apparently. Margot plans to see if she can find work there.' She sighed, then said, 'Oh, I almost forgot! Fran's on her way back from that American conference and will be spending next weekend with us. You'll have to come around and have dinner with us on Saturday.'

'That will be lovely.'

But once she'd left Elana found herself wondering why she was so appalled by Niko Radcliffe's careless destruction of a man's—no, a couple's—life. Why?

She retired to the flower room behind the counter and informed a bucket filled with roses, 'Because that's the sort of man Niko Radcliffe is. Hard, arrogant, inflexible—and obviously ruthless.'

But he'd been kind to her—albeit in a very dictatorial way.

Surely he knew that the situation at Mana hadn't been Mr Percy's fault? 'Obviously not,' she said aloud, then grimaced. Anyone coming into the shop and hearing her muttering to herself would think she was crazy.

So she'd stop thinking about Count Niko Radcliffe and get on with her life.

He meant nothing to her. *Nothing...* Although to her shame she'd dreamed of him several times since he'd delivered her home, waking after each turbulent dream with a strange sensation of loss.

Common sense warned her to be sensible. He might look like some romantic adolescent's idea of a heroic figure, and it was completely unfair that he also had charisma enough to melt an iceberg, but, unfortunately, his impact wasn't just based on physical appeal. Clearly he possessed the intelligence and determination to carve a fortune for himself in the cut-throat world of international commerce, so he must always have possessed that compelling—and disturbing—presence.

Allowing herself to drift into romantic fantasies about him would be more than stupid—it would be idiocy. She'd vowed to never again let a man like her father into her life. Although she might not be able to discipline her dreams, she could banish Niko from her mind while she was awake.

On Saturday afternoon Fran called in to catch up before Elana's dinner engagement with the Nixons that evening. 'Because of course I can't ask you all the questions I want to with the parents listening,' she informed Elana as they sat outside with coffee.

Sunlight warmed the bricks of the terrace Steve had built to catch the afternoon light, shimmered across the estuary below. For once there was no breeze to toss the blooms in the flowerbeds Elana's mother had planted.

Fran sighed. 'Sometimes I dream of this when I'm away, and I wonder why I ever left Waipuna. Now, tell me all about the Count, as Mum insists on calling him.'

She listened intently while Elana sketchily told her of the accident, and said, 'So you spent the night at Mana homestead with him?'

'And the housekeeper,' Elana pointed out crisply.

'I bet she went off to her own quarters as soon as you turned out the lights. What do you think of the man?'

Elana hesitated. But Fran was one of the few people who knew of the abuse she and her mother had suffered until they'd escaped. 'He's an alpha male, so naturally I'm not at all keen on him.'

'Not all alphas are violent like your father.'

'Intellectually I know that,' Elana admitted. 'Has your mother told you he actually sacked Greg Percy?'

'Yes.' Fran shrugged. 'Tough. But nowadays you don't—and can't—just dump workers for no reason. Possibly Mr Percy's not capable of carrying out the plans Niko Radcliffe has for Mana. If the interesting paragraphs Mum's been reading in the dentist's waiting room have any basis at all in truth—'

'Which is highly unlikely,' Elana interjected dryly.

Fran grinned. 'But possible! Whatever, I can't see Radcliffe living here, it's just too isolated. Right now his company's building a new heliport at Auckland for those who can afford to pay a lot of money to get somewhere fast. Like flying up to Mana for a secluded holiday at the homestead.'

'How do you know?'

'I read the papers,' Fran told her cheerfully. 'He's spent megabucks restoring the homestead, so turning it into a lodge makes sense.' She finished her coffee and grinned. 'Of course, you'll be in charge of decorating the house with flowers.'

Laughing, Elana said, 'I'll believe the lodge story when I see hard evidence for it.' She sobered quickly. 'I hope the new manager Niko Radcliffe's chosen doesn't get the same treatment as poor Mr Percy. His wife—Mrs West—is the housekeeper and she's lovely.'

Fran shrugged. 'Surely plutocrats have minions who deal with hiring and firing? Actually, he's got a good reputation as an employer. No migrant workers in slums are slaving away to add to his billions.'

Oddly relieved, Elana drained her coffee mug and set it down. 'Really?'

'Yes.'

'OK, he's gone up a bit in my estimation.'

'You don't think much of men, do you? Not that I blame you.' She directed a sympathetic glance at

Elana. 'Your father was a horrible man, and then you had the bad luck to fall for Roland Whatsisname. At least you got away from that affair comparatively unscathed.'

'And learnt my lesson,' Elana told her crisply.

'Do you remember your father much?'

Remember him?

Oh, yes, she remembered—a harsh voice, shouting, followed by the dreadful anguish of her mother's sobbing. He'd never struck her mother while she was present, but, child though she was, she'd known what he was doing, and she was terrified of him. Even their escape had been marred by fear that her father might find them.

Which he had.

'Yes, I remember him,' Elana said quietly.

Fran reached over and gripped her hand for a moment. 'I think that deep inside you there's still that child who's terrified of your father. Understandable, of course. You never had counselling, did you?'

'No. But I saw how Steve was with Mum. She used to groan periodically about his slapdash approach to life, but he made her—and me—really happy. He taught me to trust him.'

Her friend said, 'Good for him. But did he teach you to trust any other man?'

Elana stared at her. 'What do you mean?'

Fran shrugged. 'You might have learned to trust Steve, but has that trust extended to any other man? Your father was not normal; most men aren't brutal tyrants like him.'

'I *know* that—'

'Yes, but have you ever wondered whether perhaps you won't let yourself become attached to anyone because you're terrified they might turn into a monster like your father?'

Elana opened her mouth to protest, then closed it again. Was there any chance she might be right? Her mother had once told her that her father seemed perfectly normal before they'd married—indeed, she'd been flattered by his concern for her...

'No, I haven't,' she said crisply.

Her friend said cheerfully, 'Well, perhaps you should think abut it. Anyway, what *do* you think of Niko Radcliffe? At first Mum thought he was straight out of a fairy tale—he's practically a prince! Prince Niko—it sounds good, doesn't it?'

'Why isn't he a prince? Why is he just a Count?'

Fran sighed. 'In San Mari they stick to keeping the power in male hands. His mother was a princess, but she married a commoner so he's a Count—and in San Mari that's the equivalent of a royal duke. What do you think of him?'

Elana shrugged. 'He responds to an emergency with a cool head and plenty of orders, and he's also very strong. He dragged Jordan out of the car and carried him to safety, and Jordan's no light weight.' She stopped before adding, 'Also, he's arrogant.'

Fran's brows shot up. 'How?'

'Well, after interfering Phil Jacobs told him about Mum and Steve and the accident, he practically kidnapped me.'

'I'd call that a strong protective instinct.' Fran grinned at the expression on Elana's face. 'I like that in a man. And I like that he organised a chaperone for you.'

Elana snorted. 'I don't like that he sacked poor Greg Percy.'

Fran sobered. 'You don't know the reason. Niko Radcliffe's known to be a tough negotiator, but he's well-respected. He must have a good reason for sacking Mr Percy.'

'The only reason I can think of is that he blamed him for the state of Mana Station.' Elana shrugged. 'Which is totally unfair—Mr Percy did his best even though the owners drained it of money.'

'I wonder why he stayed there, then? Surely he could have got a better job managing a farm somewhere else?'

Surprised, Elana paused. 'Perhaps he just liked living here?'

'Perhaps it was an easy option. And you're very willing to believe the worst of Radcliffe,' Fran pointed out. 'Your mother's experience with your father was dreadful, and your affair with Roland must have only reinforced your fears. But your mother got over it and married Steve. I truly don't think you have.'

'Of course I've got over it,' Elana told her trenchantly.

'Then why are you so wary about any sort of relationship? Apart from Roland Pearson, has any other man made your heart go pitter-patter?'

'Well, there was Craig Brown in high school—'

Fran grinned. 'He revved up everybody's heartbeat, that one.' Then she assumed a prim face. 'I meant, of course, since you became an adult.'

Actually, yes. Two. One narrow escape, and the other—well, Niko Radcliffe not only set her heart racing, but alerted every cell in her body, a reaction compounded of fiery awareness and a dangerously disturbing adrenalin rush.

Fortunately her experience with Roland had taught her not to fall for macho charisma. Both touched and exasperated, she said quietly, 'A pitter-pattering heart means nothing more than that—for some purely physical reason—you find someone attractive.'

'Do you think you'll ever trust a man enough to allow him to get close to you?'

'Fran, I'm all *right*.' She eyed her best friend with mingled exasperation and affection. 'OK, so physical attraction is an important part of falling in love, but it's not *the* most important thing. I'm not over the hill yet—I'm twenty-four, the same age as you! And it's not as though I'm a blushing virgin.'

'I agree with you, marriage is a serious business.' Fran leaned forward, and touched Elana's arm. 'I know you can have a good life without marrying or falling in love, but it's—well, it's cowardly to let your mother's experience darken your own life.' She paused. 'You're intelligent and sensible—intellectually you must know that most men are not abusers. You just need to give the terrified kid that's still hiding deep inside you a chance to act on that knowledge.'

Elana opened her mouth, only to close it as Fran went on, 'OK, OK, I know when I've said enough. Tell me, how's your work going?' Before Elana could answer she said sternly, 'I don't mean the florist's shop. You did a brilliant job with the book the museum put out for the centenary of the hall. It must have taken ages—I hope they paid you for your work.'

'I got expenses,' Elana said a little defensively.

Fran's brows shot up. 'I should jolly well think so!'

'I'm hoping to be able to give up working in the shop soon. After the first article I did for the local newspaper I was contacted by a couple of people who wanted me to interview their relatives. I really enjoyed it, and they paid well, and I'm getting more requests now, some even from the South Island. I've turned those down because I can't get away for long enough to do it, but it's fascinating to interview people.'

Fran leaned forward. 'If you were based somewhere central—Auckland, Hamilton, perhaps—it would be a lot more convenient for you.'

'So far I'm finding plenty to write about in

Northland. Anyway, with Auckland's property market going berserk, I couldn't afford to buy or even rent there now. And I know Mum hoped I'd stay here for a while.'

'Why?'

Elana hesitated, pain gripping her. Steadying her voice, she went on, 'She wanted me to keep the place where she and Steve had been so happy, but—I don't want to leave. Not yet, anyway.'

Fran reached out and squeezed Elana's tightly clenched hand. 'I think I understand. Coming to live here, and for the first time in your life being happy and feeling safe, must make Waipuna mean a lot to you.'

Elana nodded. Selling the house would be like tearing her heart out, bidding an irrevocable farewell to almost everything that was good and worthwhile in her life.

Fran released her hand. 'Then that's all that matters.' She grinned. 'You know, when you meet the next man who sets your heartbeat jumping, I think you need to trust yourself enough to at least get to know him.'

'What if he's fifty?'

When she'd finished laughing, Fran told her,

'I'm not ageist. Mind you, attached men are emphatically not on the menu.'

'Of course.' Elana hesitated, then shrugged. 'OK, I'll try it. Just don't expect miracles.'

'I'm not.' Fran glanced at her watch. 'And if I'm to buy the food Mum wants to cook for dinner tonight, I'd better go now.'

After she'd waved goodbye, Elana looked around her house, the cottage that Steve and her mother had transformed from a basic shack to a home.

She walked out onto the terrace, stopping to gaze across the estuary, its surface unruffled and gleaming, the ancient trees on the hills over the far side glowing in shades ranging from olive to a shimmering golden green in the spring sun.

Did she unconsciously view all men as a threat? If so, no wonder she'd found the few times she'd had sex with Roland to be embarrassing and without pleasure. She'd thought her lack of passion was due to an inherent coldness.

And she did understand that most men were like her stepfather—kind, practical, and capable of making the right woman as happy as her mother had been in her second marriage.

So based on past experience—and once Niko

Radcliffe was safely on the other side of the world—it wasn't likely she'd have to monitor her heart rate anxiously for any betraying surges.

CHAPTER FIVE

ELANA WINCED AS the fire station alarm shrieked a summons to the local volunteers. She peered through the shop windows to the street outside. It had rained during the night so it probably wasn't a scrub fire. A car accident? Pray heaven it wasn't a house fire...

Which reminded her that she had to contact her bank. After hearing a suspicious rattle in the roof a couple of days ago she'd called in the local expert, who'd fixed it, then warned her the whole place needed reroofing some time soon.

'How much will that cost?' she'd asked.

The sum the roofer quoted still made her feel queasy. She'd have to borrow the money. Adding to her concern, only that morning Mrs Nixon had informed her with a worried face that she'd heard an out-of-towner was considering setting up another florist's business in Waipuna.

'They'll be silly,' she'd said. 'Waipuna's really not big enough for two florists.'

No, indeed. Competition could mean that Rosalie, the owner of the shop, might have to downsize...which would almost certainly mean that Elana would lose her job.

Frowning, she turned to check the order book.

Yes, the customer *had* specified orange Peruvian lilies for her daughter-in-law's bouquet. Fervently hoping that the recipient liked the colour, Elana went into the back room to assemble them, only to be immediately interrupted by the warning buzz of the shop bell. Summoning a welcoming smile, she went out.

And suffered an explosion of heartbeats when her startled gaze met ice-blue eyes in a hard, handsome face. Her smile froze on her lips.

Niko's black brows lifted. 'Hello, Elana,' he said smoothly. 'Don't look so startled. If I remember correctly, I did mention that I intended to visit Mana reasonably often.'

Mouth suddenly dry, she said, 'I'm sure you remember correctly. How are you?'

'Very well, thank you.' His tone was amused. 'And you?'

'Oh, fine.' She produced another smile and added, 'Thank you,' before turning. 'I'll just put these flowers back into water.'

Which gave her a brief ten seconds to get away from that challenging gaze and control the jumble of impressions flashing through her brain. In the couple of weeks he'd been away Niko Radcliffe's formidable, controlled authority seemed to have become even stronger and more uncompromising than she remembered.

And her stupid heart was going berserk in her chest. It took an effort of will to quell the urge to press her clenched fist there in a futile attempt to rein in that remorseless thudding.

Everything—the sunshine on the street outside, the fresh perfume of mingled greenery and flowers inside the shop, the cold blue of Niko Radcliffe's gaze, the ironic curve to his sinfully sculpted mouth—suddenly sang to her, the colours more vivid, their impact physical, a joyous assault on her senses. Something sweet and wild burst into life within her, every muscle tensing in a sharp pang of anticipation as she stuffed the lilies back into the vase, took a deep breath, and returned to the shop.

'There, that's done,' she said inanely, hoping her voice sounded prosaic and very normal.

His brows shot up. 'Not a subtle colour, those

flowers. Presumably they're for a colour-blind recipient.'

'They're popular because in a hospital ward they glow like sunlight.'

And immediately regretted her crisp tone. She sounded like a schoolmistress cautioning a child. *Stop this right now. Breathe slowly.*

His brows lifted, but he returned calmly, 'I suppose they do. I want to send flowers to England.'

Elana picked up the pen, found the right form, and looked up enquiringly, but before she could ask for details he handed her a piece of paper. 'Everything you need is there.'

It was. No gorgeous film star or princess— these flowers would go to Lady Sophia Double-Barrelled-Name who lived in a manor house somewhere in England.

So *calm down*, she warned her jumping heart. *That heavy thudding—it's just overreaction. Not only is he way, way out of your league, but he's already committed.*

'Any specific date for them to arrive?' she asked.

'No.'

Niko knew that, sophisticated and experienced as she was, Sophia would recognise the flowers for what they were—a civilised farewell after he'd ended their affair.

Elana looked up, her expression guarded. 'I'll get that off straight away.'

For some reason her tone exasperated him. The only time he'd seen her without that armour of self-possession was when they'd met in the hall at Mana after the accident.

Inconveniently, an image of sultry, shadowed eyes of green-gold and sinuous curves clad in an over-sized nightgown that revealed too much silken skin played across his mind.

As it had far too often since he'd last seen Elana Grange...

Ignoring the memory, he handed her his credit card, forcing himself to concentrate on her hands as she processed it. They were slender and deft, the nails clipped and clean. Ignoring a stray and extremely suggestive thought, he asked, 'Before I left Waipuna Mrs Nixon informed me you wrote the centennial publication on Waipuna's history.'

'Yes,' she said as though admitting a minor crime.

'And that you write articles for an historical magazine.'

After a surprised glance she nodded.

'Then you'll probably be interested in the discovery of boxes and crates of what seem to be discarded documents and old newspapers in the attic, and more in what was once the stables at Mana.'

Her face lit up. 'Really? I wish I'd known that when I took on the centennial book.'

'I've had a quick look at some of the accessible stuff, mostly from the late nineteenth century. There are diaries written by various members of the family who owned it then. It looks as though they never threw anything away.'

'Oh, that's amazing,' she breathed, sounding like someone discovering buried treasure. 'I'm surprised—and so glad—the previous owner didn't burn everything, or dump it. I wonder what else has been abandoned there?'

'Plenty,' Niko told her dryly. 'Why didn't the family who sold the place to them remove their own belongings?'

'The family died out—there was no one to inherit. The station was sold as is, and the money went to charity.' Elana gave him a quick smile, not quite meeting his eyes. 'What are you planning to do with the records?'

'Not burn everything in sight,' he said dryly,

and watched her relax. 'I'm going to employ someone to go through it and catalogue the lot. I don't know what's important and what's not. I believe you've done quite a bit of that sort of thing.'

'I—yes,' she admitted.

'I'm offering you the job.'

Her eyes widened, their exotic radiance emphasised by the gold speckles lighting the dark green depths.

Seductive as hell. Deep inside Niko something feral tightened into intense hunger.

In a far from seductive tone, she said, 'It would take me quite a while—I can't give up my job here.'

'I believe it's part-time only.'

'Full-time at the moment—Rosalie, who owns the shop, is in Australia.'

'I presume she's not planning to settle there?'

That drew a reluctant smile. 'No, she's there for the birth of her first grandchild.'

'When will she be back?'

'In a fortnight if the baby arrives on time.'

Niko had expected her swift agreement. According to Mrs Nixon, the fount of all knowledge, Elana's parents had left her with nothing but the house, and her part-time position in the shop couldn't pay very well.

So why was she unwilling? He said, 'Mrs Nixon assures me you're very competent, and after reading the history you wrote, I agree with her. I also like your writing.'

This drew a startled glance. 'I enjoyed doing it. It's just—it did take up a lot of time. And the documents I used were already catalogued.'

'You are a librarian, so I presume you know how to catalogue.'

'Well, yes,' she returned, her reluctance obvious.

'I will, of course, pay you.'

She hesitated, her expression freezing a moment as though something had just occurred to her. Whatever it was, it decided her. 'No, I'm afraid it's just not convenient right now.' Again she paused, before saying, 'I can give you the name of a friend who does this sort of thing for a living—he's very good, and much more experienced than I am.'

How good a friend? Startled by the intensity of that primitive reaction, Niko reined in an instant, angry speculation and said, 'But you're right here, and you have background knowledge that will help.'

'Well, yes,' she agreed, frowning. 'But—'

'Also, you have a fervent advocate in Mrs Nixon.' He added dryly, 'She told me all about your skill at interviewing.'

Elana's smile held wry humour. 'That's not really a recommendation. Mrs Nixon has a wide knowledge of the district as well as an excellent memory.'

Her lips tightened momentarily before easing into their normal ripe contours. Memories of her mouth had bothered him...so seductively feminine, a mouth made for sensuous kisses and softly passionate words, lips that contrasted intriguingly with the inner strength he sensed in her, the way she kept her emotions under strict control. In a way, he could blame those lips for sending him back to England to tell Sophia that their affair was over.

Hunger stirred his body, a fierce need that was becoming familiar. He was long past the wilful, almost uncontrollable desire of adolescence, so although Elana's rejection of his offer was irritating, it should be no big deal.

Yet even now, he found himself wondering what it would take to breach the barriers he sensed within her.

Smooth words? Luxury? The promise of passion?

Or money?

Fighting a silent battle, Elana wished he'd go away. Why didn't she agree, just thank fate for sending her this opportunity? She needed money to repair the roof.

Apart from that, it would be a fascinating project.

She was a coward.

No, darn it, she was being sensible!

She deeply mistrusted the heady rush of sensation that had raced through every cell in her body when Niko walked into the shop. Everything about him was vividly, thrillingly familiar, as though she'd carried him in her heart since she'd last seen him.

Seeing too much—no, *anything*—of him was going to cause chaos to her peace of mind.

But then he wasn't likely to be in New Zealand often, or for any length of time. After a few taut moments, and as warily as though she was taking a huge step into unknown danger, she said quietly, 'I can't give you a decision so quickly. I am working full-time here until Rosalie gets back.'

Bracing herself, she met his narrowed gaze steadily, trying to suppress a sudden twist of tantalising, sharp sensation deep inside her.

Niko wasn't a man who'd suffer second best; he'd expect perfection. Could she deliver?

'Think it over,' he said calmly. 'I'll call you when I get back from Auckland in a couple of days and you can give me your answer.'

She watched him stride out of the shop, a formidable figure in jeans and a checked shirt. No doubt, she decided cynically as she turned towards the back room, it helped that those casual clothes had probably been created by some brilliant tailor who knew exactly how to make the most of broad shoulders, lean hips and long, strongly muscled legs.

And clearly he was totally confident that he'd persuade her.

Stop obsessing about the man! Her traitor heart might still be jumping, but she was afraid. Niko Radcliffe affected her in so many ways, he could be disaster central.

* * *

The next evening after a day of showers and her discovery of another ominous stain in the ceiling, she checked her computer and to her dismay found that disaster central actually looked to be the combination of a dodgy roof and a cautious bank that didn't feel it could lend her the money to fix the roof.

Trying to calm her nerves by watching the news, she discovered that she'd been wrong about that too. Disaster could well be lurking in a storm forming far to the north in heated equatorial waters.

Gaze fixed on the ominous whirlpool symbol on the screen, Elana found herself holding her breath, hoping that it wouldn't go near any of the islands that scattered the tropical sea.

And cravenly, that it would stay well away from New Zealand.

She switched off the television and walked across to the window, narrowing her eyes against the westering sun that shone from an almost cloudless sky, sheening the water with silver.

Actually, she had no option. She had to take on the job of organising all those documents. As soon as she'd confirmed that with Niko Radcliffe, she'd ring the roofer.

Her gaze ranged over the opulent amber curves of the beaches on the estuary. Beyond the river mouth a small yacht headed for safe anchorage in the Bay of Islands, and silhouetted on the horizon was a container ship making its way down the coast to Auckland. It was almost impossible to imagine something as dangerous as a tropical storm whipping those calm waters into destructive waves.

However, they happened. Cyclones were rare, but they could cause chaos and devastation even as far south as Northland.

'What next?' she asked forlornly, then frowned at her foolishness. Why was she whimpering because fate was forcing her in a direction she didn't want to go? Niko's offer couldn't have come at a better time.

It seemed unlikely she'd earn enough to entirely reroof the house, but she hoped she could convince the bank she'd be able to repay the loan.

'And if they don't agree?' she said aloud, hating the sound of the words.

If that happened, she'd have to sell the house.

She turned and looked around the room, its furniture shabby but still gracious. Here she'd learned what love between a man and woman could be, learned that a man could be tender with children. She'd discovered what it was like to feel safe.

A lump in her throat threatened to choke her. She swallowed it, and pulled the curtains. If it happened, she'd survive. She turned back into the room, her gaze lingering lovingly on the pictures her mother had painted of the estuary, and made up her mind. When Niko contacted her she'd tell him that she'd catalogue the documents. After all, she'd enjoy doing it.

So why on earth had she been behaving like a drama queen?

Self-preservation, she thought starkly. Every female instinct she possessed was shouting that the more she saw of Niko, the more dangerously he affected her.

She said aloud, 'All I have to do is remind myself that his life and mine might as well be on different planets.'

Immediately, before she could change her mind, she rang the roofer. Ten minutes later she got off the phone, sighing with relief. At last something was going right—he'd be able to do the job within days, airily dismissing her concern about not paying him immediately. 'No problem, Elana. I know you'll get there. You were always a conscientious kid.'

In her fourth year at Waipuna School his wife had been her teacher. Life in a small community might occasionally seem stifling, but it had good points too, she thought wryly.

That night she wooed slumber with a singular lack of success.

Fortunately the morning sun radiated a summery promise from a cloudless sky. Her spirits lifted as she inhaled the fresh, herbal scent of the costal forest on the road into Waipuna. She had quite a busy day ahead, but no customers disturbed her for just over an hour until the buzz of the shop bell summoned her from the chiller room.

So of course the person who waited for her had to be Niko Radcliffe, and her idiotic heart had to lose control again.

'Oh—hello,' she said inanely.

Blue eyes scanned her with far too much intimidating speculation. 'What's the matter?'

'Nothing,' she returned, straightening her shoulders and lifting her chin.

'You look tired.'

She ignored the comment. 'I'll catalogue those documents.'

Black brows lifted and his mouth hardened. 'I'm sorry to put you through enough trauma to make this such a difficult decision,' he said.

Sarcastic beast!

'I'm worried about this possible cyclone,' she told him stonily. 'Big storms play havoc with flowers. Most of ours come from Auckland, which will be at risk if the wretched cyclone makes it this far south.'

'We're all concerned about that.'

Why should it bother him? If the storm tracked too close to Northland he could just climb into his helicopter and fly off to his huge station in the South Island where he'd be safe...

Trying to sound brisk, Elana said, 'With any luck it will get lost on the way and end up dying a natural death somewhere on the way to Chile.'

'Let's hope so.'

She nodded. 'I sometimes wonder if the emergency organisations tend to overstate the strength of storms so people won't be idiots and push their luck.'

'Only to have some do just that in spite of all the warnings,' he observed dryly.

As Steve had done. His decision not to wear a seatbelt had killed him.

Niko watched her features harden, her mouth tighten. Why? Although she seemed aware of him, she clearly didn't want anything from him. Did she have an inherent distrust of him—or was it all men?

Perhaps she'd been badly hurt by an affair gone wrong.

And why did he find Elana Grange so attractive—OK, dammit, so intensely desirable? All he should want from her was her expertise at dealing with documents. Yet he couldn't overcome or banish this inconvenient, tantalising tug of sensual hunger.

Too abruptly he asked, 'What changed your mind?'

Elana certainly wasn't going to admit to a shortage of money. 'I surrendered to temptation,' she told him, not hiding the irony in her tone. 'All those documents—who knows what fascinating things I might find in them?'

'Possibly little more than boring day-to-day incidents,' he observed cynically. 'Now we talk money.' And named a sum that made her blink.

'That's far too much,' she blurted.

'Nonsense. It's the going rate.'

'Are you sure?' she demanded.

He gave her a look that silenced her. 'You agreed to do it. I'm holding you to that. You'll have to fit it in around your hours here, which will mean weekend work for you. Naturally you'll earn extra for that.'

'But—'

He interrupted smoothly, 'I suggest you start by spending a couple of days checking out the documents and making notes. I'll see you tomorrow morning.'

Taken aback, Elana said, 'No, it's Saturday, and the shop doesn't close until one.'

He frowned. 'Come directly to Mana after you've closed the shop and I'll show you where most of the documents are.'

It sounded like an order. Stiffly Elana responded, 'Very well, Mr Radcliffe. Or should I say, *Aye, aye, sir*?'

Niko's exasperation warred with wry amusement. He deserved it. 'Neither. I didn't intend to sound officious, and my name is Niko.'

After giving him a startled glance, she half smiled. 'Very well, Niko, I'll be there around two o'clock.'

Whenever she said it, his name sounded different on her lips. What would it sound like if she were in his arms? Would her voice deepen, turn husky, slur...?

Ruthlessly shutting down that train of thought, he said, 'I suggest you spend at least a couple of days—longer if it's necessary—going through the boxes and crates and making notes.' He glanced at his watch. 'Until tomorrow, then.'

Elana watched him turn and leave the shop, relieved at being able to breathe again. But she dragged her gaze away when he stopped outside to greet a woman she didn't recognise—rather glamorous but a little too overdressed for Waipuna.

Startled by that swift snide judgment, Elana strode into the flower room. She'd never before met a man like Niko Radcliffe—and never would be too soon to meet another one. His potent male magnetism set her foolish heart throbbing, but, more significantly, he was beginning to invade her mind, turning her into someone who'd just unkindly judged a woman she'd never seen before.

That night the television forecaster charted the progress of the weather system far in the north, still not an official cyclone, but already creating havoc in the tropical islands it crossed. Elana tried to read a library book, which failed utterly to capture her attention; every time she turned a page she somehow saw Niko's face superimposed over the print. Disgusted by her foolishness, she gave up and headed for bed.

The next day a radiant sky and the complete lack of wind mocked any fears of the weather. As she negotiated the cattle stop between the stone walls—now as pristine as when they'd first been built—she tried to discipline her jumping heartbeat. Infuriatingly, it began to race when she pulled to a stop outside the gates. She grabbed her bag from the passenger seat beside her and opened the door.

When she straightened up and turned, Niko

was striding towards her, the sun striking blue flames from his black hair. Clad in a casual polo shirt and jeans, he moved with a dangerous litheness that sent erotic little shivers scudding down her spine.

Hoping her involuntary, reckless response was well hidden, she forced a smile and said sedately, 'Good afternoon.'

'Good afternoon. Would you like coffee before we start?'

We start? Surely not...

Her reply was crisp. 'No, thank you. I'll get to work.'

'Before you do, come and have a look at something Patty West found in the attic this morning.'

'What is it?'

'Watercolours of the garden. Amateurish—probably painted by family members, and, judging by the clothes, I'd say late nineteenth century.'

The difference between its previous musty disrepair and the elegance that greeted her when she went into the homestead once more took Elana's breath away. It was a joy to see the house resplendently celebrating its many years with pride and grace.

'I'm so glad you brought this place back to life,' she told her host.

He shrugged. 'The architect and the work-men—and the decorator—have done a very good job.'

Not surprising. His ruthless dismissal of Mana's previous manager proved that Count Niko Rad-cliffe had no time for people who failed to meet his standards. If he didn't think she was earning her wage he'd almost certainly sack her as bru-tally as he'd ditched Mr Percy.

He went on, 'The house was well-built origi-nally, and the framework is still good. Only the roof had to be replaced—by the same man who tells me he's expecting to do yours soon.'

Startled, and more than a little annoyed, Elana could only say, 'Oh—yes.'

His smile held more irony than amusement. 'Living in a small country area has plenty of ad-vantages, but I'm sure you understand privacy isn't one of them.'

'Indeed I do,' she said briskly, and changed the subject. 'What are your plans for the garden? Some of the trees look pretty dilapidated. I hope none of them are too far gone to be saved.'

'Relax,' he said, smiling. 'I've been advised of

a good arborist and I'll only agree to sacrificing trees that are a danger. The drawings are out on the veranda.'

He'd spread them out on a table, and stood by as Elana perused them carefully, eyes half-closed against the brilliance of the afternoon sun on the waters of the estuary.

'They're charming.' She scanned a border the artist had delineated carefully. 'Whoever did this studied the plants minutely.'

'If you come across more as you go through the documents, I've organised an expert in conservation for them. My PA has given me a sheet of contacts for you.'

Elana's upward glance met cool blue eyes. She forgot what she'd been intending to say as warmth spread through her, quickening her breath, setting her traitor heart pounding in her ears.

Even her voice sounded odd as she said, 'Thank you.'

Here at Mana, Niko Radcliffe beside her, she was suddenly gripped by an overwhelming sense of belonging, as though she'd been lost and was found, as though somehow the scattered parts of her life were reassembling—not as they had been before, but forming a different pattern, making her whole once more.

As though once, long ago, she'd stood here with this man beside her, looking out over the garden towards the estuary...

She felt strangely, dangerously secure. Bewildered, she wrenched her gaze away from his narrowed survey and focused on the watercolours.

Of course nothing momentous had happened. Struggling to summon some practical common sense, she told herself that those few moments of rightness, of belonging, had to be a flash of *déjà vu,* the occasional startling sensation of reliving a forgotten, or never experienced, occasion.

In other words, her brain was playing tricks on her. So she'd ignore it.

Niko startled her by asking abruptly, 'What's happened? Are you all right?'

'I'm fine.' She blinked, keeping her gaze on the faded pictures. 'I wonder what else has been abandoned.' And went on, 'I'm sure you've got other things to do. If you point me in the direction of the stables, I'll have a look around there.'

'I'll take you there,' he said.

Firmly.

* * *

When her teeth closed a second on her bottom lip Niko had to prevent himself from telling her to stop ravaging her soft mouth.

And from wondering exactly how it would feel if she ever nipped his skin...

As his whole body responded to the wayward thought, he cursed silently. This was ridiculous. It was just as well he was leaving Waipuna; his body was betraying him with a lack of discretion he hadn't experienced since his adolescence. Yes, Elana was attractive and intelligent, independent and self-possessed—all things he found desirable in a woman. But this hunger, this wild need was nothing he'd experienced before. Why *this* woman?

Elana looked up, met an intent, hard gaze that sent a scary excitement down her spine, mixed with an even scarier anticipation.

Niko said, 'Before we go to the stables, I'll show you where you'll be working.'

He'd organised an office for her in the homestead, a small room off the veranda. 'Check the equipment,' he ordered. 'My personal assistant said you'll need all this, but take a look. If anything else is necessary it will be supplied.'

After a swift survey of the room she said, 'No, your PA knew exactly what I'd need.'

He told her ironically, 'She knows exactly what anyone needs. In some ways she reminds me very much of Mrs Nixon.'

Elana laughed. 'Then she must have a heart of gold.'

Niko found himself warming to that laughter—it was spontaneous and fresh, close to mischievous. This was a different side to Elana—one he hadn't suspected. Until then she'd been guarded, keeping her emotions controlled and corralled beneath that cool composure.

Her spontaneity touched some part of him, summoning a sudden query. What would she be like as a lover?

Would that spontaneity extend to her caresses, to her kisses? Another charge of hunger, of sheer, potent need, shot through him like a jolt of electricity.

Dangerous—and definitely *not* something he wanted to happen.

Frowning, he looked out of the window. 'I'll

see that the garden bed out there is tidied up so you have a decent outlook instead of a tangle of creepers and shrubs and weeds.'

'I rather like it,' she told him, touched by his consideration. 'It's very like Sleeping Beauty's garden—oh, and look, there's an early rose.'

'Roses are your favourite flowers?'

A little surprised, she smiled. 'They're just about everyone's, aren't they?'

He sent her a quizzical glance. 'Judging by your tone, not yours?'

'When I was a little girl I loved aquilegias— the flowers my mother called Granny's Bonnets. They were purple and they fitted over the end of my finger like a little cap. The bumblebees loved them. And I have to admit to falling deeply for those great, flaunting crimson blooms on some magnolia trees.'

'How about huge fluffy pink peonies?'

'Love them too,' she said promptly. 'They won't grow here, of course. They need much colder winters.'

Like the ones in the Southern Alps, where he'd been born.

His question brought her back to some sort of

equilibrium. He'd gone from a high country station to a palace and a title. She might be acutely, *desperately* aware of him, but when he decided to marry he'd almost certainly choose someone who'd fit into his life.

Marry? Where on earth had that thought come from?

She forced herself to meet his penetrating gaze. 'How do you want me to report to you?'

And held her breath until he said, 'I don't know how long I'll be away. I have a business deal to close in China. Email me periodically with your progress. No, better still, we'll use the computer's communications programme so we can talk. You know how to do that?' He watched as she nodded, and added, 'I'll email you with dates and times. And don't hurry. I don't care how long you take—just do a good job.'

Which sounded simple, but after seeing the cartons of documents, Elana realised just how much time she might need to spend at Mana.

Niko said a formal goodbye when the chopper arrived; equally formally she wished him a safe journey. But the homestead seemed oddly empty and echoing after he'd gone.

Now, coping with this unexpected, bewildering hunger for a man she knew so little about, she had to be grateful for her mother's hard-won wisdom when it came to charismatic men.

Yet, in a way she didn't understand, the very intensity of feelings evoked by Niko's presence had somehow broken through the numbing grief that had shadowed her emotions these past months.

Was it a stage in recovery, a step to reclaiming her life?

She grimaced. Not likely. Her powerful reaction to him had to be nothing more than lust. A charismatic, compelling man, he just happened to be around while she was going through perhaps the final stage of recovery from grief. And the unexpected and cryptic *déjà vu* moment in the garden must have been brought on by memories of a happy visit as a child to the homestead.

That evening the forecast brought relief. The tropical storm had turned to the right and was heading out across the Pacific, losing intensity as it sank into cooler latitudes, and well away from both New Zealand and the islands of Polynesia to the north.

'But there's a nasty low sneaking up from the

South Pole,' the announcer informed her in an appropriately grave tone. 'It will bring winds and heavy rain to the South Island when it arrives in a couple of days. Farmers, you'll need to check the shelter for your stock, and it might pay to make sure you have stores of food, as if it keeps this intensity roads may be closed by snow in the south, or flooding further north.'

'Oh, joy,' Elana muttered caustically, and switched to another channel.

CHAPTER SIX

THE SHRILL SUMMONS of the telephone woke Elana from her first sleep. Blinking, wondering if she'd dreamt it, she peered through the darkness. Another urgent ring convinced her she was awake—and in the middle of the night this had to be an emergency. Alarm knotting her stomach, she staggered out into the sitting room and lifted the receiver. 'Hello,' she croaked.

His voice harsh, Niko said, 'Sorry to wake you but I've just seen your car being driven towards Waipuna.'

'Wha—*what?*' She drew in a dazed breath, convinced she was dreaming. 'Niko? No, you're in China.'

'Not now, I'm back in Waipuna.'

They'd spoken every day since he'd left a fortnight previously, and each time his face on the computer screen had charged her with excitement—futile and foolish excitement. He'd shown interest in her progress with the documents, and he'd spoken briefly of his impressions of Beijing, but she knew better than to build hopeless dreams.

'You didn't hear it being taken?' he asked.

'No. I'll ring the police,' she told him numbly.

'I've already done that. I'll be at your place in a few minutes.'

Heart banging, she put down the receiver. Her car was vital; without it she'd be unable to get to Waipuna to work, unable to go anywhere. Steve's old banger was still in the garage, but it didn't have a warrant of fitness and probably wouldn't get one without quite a lot of money being spent on it.

'Oh, hell!' she muttered. 'Think positively, for heaven's sake. The police will stop them and they'll return the car.'

But the combination of an adrenalin overdose with a sense of violation made her feel sick. She stood staring blindly out across the estuary, until she abruptly realised she was clad in a sketchy pair of pyjamas—and Niko was on his way.

She ran to her bedroom and scrambled into jeans and a shirt, sliding her feet into the nearest footwear—a pair of sandals.

Only just in time. A beam of light swept across

the window. Feeling as though she'd been hit by a train, she raced to the door and opened it, letting out a sheet of warm light as Niko got out of the car and strode up the path towards her.

He looked like something out of a dream, tall and lithe and handsome. No prince from a fairy tale, though—his face was set in hard lines of anger.

'Where did you see the car?' she asked baldly, stepping back to let him in.

'About a kilometre down the road, heading towards Waipuna. Don't worry—the police will stop them before they get to the intersection.'

Appalled, she said, 'I hope no one gets hurt.'

'Your old schoolmate should have convinced you that the police know what they're doing in situations like this.'

He examined her keenly, trying to ignore the swift, reckless rush of hunger setting his body alight. She'd obviously scrambled into her clothes without bothering with underwear. Although her green-gold eyes were still heavy-lidded and slumbrous, she held her soft mouth under tight control, managing to look both determined and profoundly sensuous.

As she had every day when he'd contacted her. He should have emailed her instead of testing his ability to resist this sensuous attraction. Emails were safe and emotionless. Seeing her smile at him from the computer screen had only intensified his desire for her, eating away at his self-control.

He'd missed her. Right now he was gripped by an emotion he'd never experienced before— a sense of rightness, of finding his way, of—of homecoming...

Dismissing such a sentimental thought, he said abruptly, 'Whoever took your car abandoned their own vehicle—probably a stolen one—on the corner just before your gate. Either it's broken down, or they ran it out of petrol.'

Elana winced and stood back. 'I heard nothing. Thanks for ringing me.' After a moment's hesitation she said more sturdily, 'I'll let you know what happens.'

It was a definite dismissal.

Tough. Niko had no intention of leaving her. She was trying hard to sound fiercely independent, but her face was white and she needed support. He said, 'I told the police I'd stay here until they contacted you.' Ignoring her startled expression, he turned to scan what he could see of the garden. 'Where do you keep the car?'

'In the carport—up the drive a bit.' She gestured towards a tumbledown shed some distance towards the road.

'So that's why you didn't hear it going.'

Suddenly vulnerable, Elana hid a shiver at the thought of sleeping while someone stole her car. 'You don't have to stay—'

He interrupted, 'We've already had this conversation.'

'What?'

His smile was sardonic. 'The night we met. Let me in. I'm not leaving here until we know what's happened. Do you have any other vehicles?'

'Yes. My stepfather's car.' She drew a deep breath. 'I need a cup of coffee. What would you like—coffee or tea?' Although her voice was level, he could tell it took an effort.

'Coffee, thank you.' He asked tersely, 'You've got insurance?'

'Comprehensive.'

Clearly she wasn't going to confide in him. Well, why should she? Their computer conversations had been face to face, but they'd both carefully avoided any intimacy. As for this elemental hunger raging through him—hell, any man would respond to the gentle swell of her breasts beneath her loose cotton T-shirt and the curve of her buttocks as she turned into the house.

Every muscle in his body flexed. Startled and chagrined, he told himself to cool down. For some bewildering reason the thought of any other man watching her and feeling this heady, sensual response affected him with a stark possessiveness as primitive as it was unexpected.

Elana had told him her home had started out as a bach, a basic holiday cottage. It showed its origins. The front door opened into a sitting room with a dining area beyond, separated by a counter from the small kitchen towards which she was heading. The sitting-room furniture looked as though it had been reclaimed from a junk shop, and the wooden dining table was an elderly, highly polished relic of Victoriana, the chairs around it a comprehensive collection of cast-offs.

Yet in spite of its near-shabbiness it was warm and cheerful, and radiated comfort. Flowers picked from the garden were arranged casually in vases, several watercolours clearly by a local artist with some talent hung on the walls, and photographs—one of Elana in cap and gown, beaming radiantly—were displayed on shelves.

The splash of water filling a kettle brought his attention back to the kitchen.

Elana turned and opened the door of an elderly refrigerator, groped inside and turned back, a jug of milk in her hand.

'Do sit down,' she said with a strained smile. 'You're too tall for this place. I'm afraid you might hit your head on the beams.'

'I'm not quite two metres tall,' he said, glancing up. 'There's plenty of room between me and the ceiling.'

It wasn't just his height Elana found overpowering—it was the whole essence of the man. And that owed little to his height, or to his wide shoulders and long legs. His strong personality made the Mediterranean good looks he'd inherited from his mother unimportant. When they'd met he'd reminded her of a warrior king, ruling by sheer force of character. Now, standing in her home, that impression was reinforced.

Abruptly she said, 'I believe your mother's country is very mountainous?'

'Yes,' he said calmly, although his eyes had narrowed slightly.

Wondering why on earth she'd blurted such a foolish observation, she turned away to take down a couple of mugs from the cupboard. 'Were the original inhabitants forced into the mountains at some time by war?'

She could hear the shrug in his voice when he answered. 'No, they chose to live there. San Mari is a beautiful place; it's close enough to the sea for the climate to be reasonably moderate, and the soil is fertile. It provided the first settlers with everything they needed, and the surrounding mountains afforded them protection from the ambitions and wars of others.'

Keep talking, she thought feverishly. *Talking means you don't have to think about how amazing he looks and how he affects you...* 'Do you know who they were?'

'They believe they're descended from the first people ever to arrive in Europe.'

Intrigued, she looked up from pouring boiling water over the coffee in the plunger. 'That's interesting.'

He shrugged. 'No. There might be some truth in their belief that they settled San Mari very early. Archaeologists have been digging in various parts of the country for years. They've made some amazing discoveries and the further they dig, the more excited they get.'

'I suppose Kiwis find this sort of thing interesting because we're such a new country.' She gave a small laugh and expanded, 'That sounds silly, as though New Zealand's just popped up from the depths of the ocean! But humans have been here for such a short time. Maori settlers arrived about eight hundred years ago, and nobody else in the world knew the place existed until two or three hundred years ago.'

'Do you think the isolation is why travelling overseas is such a rite of passage for young New Zealanders?'

Relaxing a little, Elana nodded. 'Yes—we try to get our fill of antiquities while we're experiencing the great OE. Overseas Experience,' she elaborated.

'Is that your ambition? To travel?'

'One day, yes.'

He was good at small talk, but his deep voice and penetrating eyes were undermining her composure. Glancing at the clock, Elana realised it wasn't as late as she'd thought. She willed the telephone to ring, for someone to tell her what was happening to her car.

That would break this headlong compulsion to reach out to him, the disturbing desire to connect in the most intense and compelling way. She needed to get him out of the house before she forgot that he was the scion of some ancient family famed for their wealth, and that he'd bedded some of the most beautiful women in the world.

And before she embarrassed herself by revealing, in some way, just how strongly she was affected by his compelling presence.

'Sugar?' she asked, her voice almost breaking on the word. She had to swallow before she could go on. 'And milk?'

'Neither, thanks. Like you with tea, I drink it black.'

His remark brought back memories of the night she'd spent at Mana.

And how it had felt to be in his arms, held against his chest...

Heat burned through her, and with it something akin to recklessness. He'd wanted her then.

And all that was female in her had responded, temporarily blocking out everything but the urge to surrender.

Fortunately, she'd recognised it for what it was—a sexual pull based on the primitive instinct to reproduce. And even more fortunately a spark of common sense had asserted itself before either of them could give in to it.

But desperately, dangerously, she longed to rediscover the sensations she'd felt in his arms for that brief time, that wildly exciting arousal strangely underpinned by a sense of total security.

Carefully she poured the coffee and asked, 'Would you like something to eat?'

Banal and commonplace, the small courtesy went some way to re-establishing her equilibrium.

'No, thank you.' His voice was cool, the dismissive undertone like a shower of freezing water. Her father's tone... Even when he'd been angry enough to hit her mother, he'd never raised his voice.

Elana hated it. But at least it silenced the heady clamour in her body, her tumbling thoughts.

Still tense, she handed Niko the mug and led the way into the sitting area. Once he'd finished his coffee he'd go. In the meantime, she'd stick to small talk.

'Do sit down,' she said, but he stayed standing

until she lowered herself into Steve's favourite armchair.

Once there she searched for a sensible topic, anything to take her mind off the fact that Niko was far too close to her. In the end she asked, 'Are you planning a long stay at Mana this time?'

And could have kicked herself. Hardly impersonal...

'Only a couple of weeks,' he told her crisply.

Presumably to make sure the manager he'd installed was doing his job properly. Although the brutal removal of Greg Percy had revealed a ruthlessness she found abhorrent, she had to admit that Mana Station was already looking much more prosperous.

Of course Niko was spending a lot of money to achieve that. Much more traffic—often local tradesmen's vans—went past her gate now, and from the road she could see fences being replaced and young native trees newly planted beside the small creeks that wound their way down into the estuary. Its pastures were already looking better.

Perhaps he could read her mind, because he said, 'You'll have noticed the traffic. Sorry about the dust, but that will continue until the new houses are finished.'

'Houses?' The station already had several houses on it.

Curtly he said, 'The existing houses—except for the one the manager lived in—are shacks that have had no maintenance for years. It's cheaper to knock them down and put new ones there.'

'I see. The previous owner—'

His shoulders lifted. In a voice that could have frozen Niagara Falls he said, 'The total mismanagement of the place was not entirely due to the previous *owner.*'

Which meant what? Was he blaming Greg Percy? She glanced up, met eyes of glacial blue, and decided she'd chosen the wrong topic for this conversation. 'Actually, the traffic doesn't bother me. The trees between the house and the road keep this place free of most of the dust.'

And was hugely relieved when the telephone rang. 'That must be the police,' she said hastily, scrambling up and grabbing the handset. 'Hello?'

Niko got to his feet, his gaze fixed on her face.

'Oh, hi, Phil,' she said, turning slightly away.

For some reason Niko wasn't prepared to examine, her withdrawal caused a tight stab of anger.

As though she recognised it she stiffened, then

shot him a swift glance before turning away even further. 'OK,' she said quietly. 'Are they all right?'

Damn, did that mean that the idiots who'd stolen her car had wrecked it? And why did Phil the policeman keep turning up all the time? Surely there was more than one cop in Waipuna?

Frowning, Niko saw her stance ease a little.

'Phil, I'll manage,' she said quietly. 'I've still got Steve's car. Thanks for letting me know. Say hello to Jenny, won't you?'

Who was Jenny? The cop's wife? And why the hell, Niko thought sardonically, should he care?

Because he wanted Elana.

There, he'd admitted it. He'd wanted her from the moment he'd seen her at the ball, and since that night everything he'd discovered about her— her sturdy independence, her intelligence and sense of humour, her acceptance of more grief than anyone her age should have to cope with— had increased his regard for her.

He waited while she finished her goodbyes and replaced the telephone.

She paused a few seconds as though gathering strength, then turned and said bluntly, 'The car is a mess. The two men who stole it are either drunk or high on drugs.' She paused, as though collecting her thoughts.

'And you have insurance to cover the costs of getting your car fixed.' Niko kept his voice level, refusing to make it a question.

Nodding, she covered a yawn with her hand. He thought she braced herself before she produced a smile with very little humour. 'I'm sorry—I think reaction's settling in. Thanks very much for coming in to tell me what happened.'

Yet another very definite dismissal, Niko realised, assailed again by a stab of something more than irritation. It faded when he noted ivory skin paler than normal, and that sensuous mouth compressed into a tight line. Lowered lashes shielded her eyes, making it impossible for him to read her thoughts.

Shaken by a powerful desire to protect her, he wasn't going to leave her like this. 'It was nothing,' he said calmly. 'Sit down and finish your coffee.'

The glance she directed at him glittered with irritation, but she lowered herself into the chair. 'I'm all right.'

Niko sat down opposite her, and began to ask questions about her work on the documents.

She followed his lead, and as she spoke some of the colour seeped back into her skin. After he'd drained his coffee mug he asked, 'How long is it since you used your stepfather's car?'

She gave him a baffled glance. 'A while. Why?'

'Car engines need to be used every so often.'

Elana nodded, her brow wrinkling as she calculated. After a swift glance at a calendar on the kitchen wall, she said, 'It must be about a month since I tried the engine.' After a moment's pause she added, 'It hiccupped a bit, but it started.'

'How long since it's been on the road?'

'A couple of years.' The gaze directed his way was direct and more than a little challenging. 'Why?'

'We'd better make sure it actually goes. If it doesn't, you'll have to organise transport to work tomorrow.'

She shrugged, but got to her feet. 'OK, I'll try it.'

And wasn't surprised when he stood and said, 'I'll go with you.'

Leading him along the dark path to the shed where Steve's car resided, Elana wryly recalled

Fran's observation that she liked the fact that Niko Radcliffe clearly had a strong protective attitude.

Could be, but more probably it was simply that because of his upbringing he was accustomed to telling people what to do.

The wavering light of the torch picked out her mother's herb garden and the citrus trees, each one protected by a trap from marauding possums. The waves on the beach whispered a soft background to the scent of growing things and the salty tang of the estuary, and above them stars blazed against a sky so intensely black the immensity of the universe ached through her.

In an oddly flat voice Elana said, 'Here it is,' and handed the torch over, explaining, 'There's no light in here, so if you hold it I'll try the car.'

And shivered when their fingers collided as he took the torch.

'Go ahead,' he said in the coolly dismissive tone she hated.

It was a warning—a necessary one. Otherwise the forbidden response that scudded through her might have transmuted into something infinitely more dangerous.

Once in the car, she turned the key. Apart from

a click, nothing happened. Tensely, she tried again.

Still nothing.

'The battery must be flat,' she said weakly, and twisted the key once more, willing it to work. Instead it clicked and died.

A dark form against the greater darkness of the night, Niko said, 'Possibly, or it could be the starter solenoid. Hold the torch and I'll take a look.'

What on earth was a starter solenoid? Reluctantly Elana climbed out, took the torch from him and held it while he lifted the bonnet.

'Aim it here,' he said. 'Do you have a screwdriver?'

'Screwdriver?' she asked numbly. Where had he become so familiar with the working of car engines? Not in a palace, surely.

'Yes. If it's the solenoid we'll be able to start it with a screwdriver across the points.'

'Oh. Steve kept his tools here,' she said and turned away, directing the torch to where the battered metal box should have been.

Unfortunately there was no sign of it. And for some reason this threw her more than anything else that had happened that night. The beam of light wavering across the rusty corrugated iron wall of the shed, she said in a voice she had to struggle to keep steady, 'It's not here.'

'Leave it,' Niko commanded. 'You're tired. Give me the torch.'

'I'm all *right*,' she told him abruptly.

It wasn't exhaustion that weighed her down. An overdose of adrenalin, made dangerous by a reckless, headstrong hunger, had been building swiftly since the moment she'd opened the door to him.

The conversations they'd shared while he was away had somehow sparked—or reinforced—an emotion she'd never felt before. The realisation terrified her and, in some strange way, exhilarated her too, as though she were poised on the edge of a high precipice, gazing over a beautiful, unknown landscape filled with hidden dangers.

'You're not all right. We need to get back to the house. I gave my cell-phone number to the police, but they may be trying to ring you.'

She snapped, 'I wish you'd stop telling me how I feel. And what to do.' And had to stop herself from finishing petulantly, *I'm the best judge of what I want.*

Only to realise with stunned shock and a surge

of blatant anticipation that what she wanted right now was Niko Radcliffe. In every way...

Wanted him so much it actually *hurt*.

She dragged in a deep breath, but no longed-for serenity washed through her; she still throbbed with that hungry, terrifying need.

Niko reached into the car and removed the keys, then straightened to walk to the front of the car and lower the bonnet. And startled her by saying coolly as he straightened, 'I'm sorry.'

For some reason that brought a reluctant smile to her lips. Hastily banishing it, she said, 'You're going to have to produce a little more contrition than that to make me believe you.'

He laughed, and for a poignant second she saw the mischievous boy he must once have been. Her shaky defences crumbled into nothingness, and she took a step towards him, only to realise from the sudden hardening of his face what she was inviting.

'Take care, it's a bit uneven here,' she told him jerkily, and swivelled to direct the warm light of the torch away from him to the path.

By the time they reached the house she'd re-gained enough control to say, 'Thanks for that. I'll see if I've got a screwdriver—'

'Don't worry,' he said levelly. 'There's bound to be one in my car.'

She swallowed. 'It doesn't matter—'

'You might as well know what the problem is with that car.' He stopped and held out his hand. 'Give me the torch. You're shivering. Go inside— you don't need to stay out here.'

She opened her mouth to protest, then thought better of it. Away from him she'd have time to regroup, return to her usual equilibrium, scotch this impetuous, crazy longing for something— something *dangerous*, something that might mark her for life if she surrendered to it.

'All right,' she said, carefully avoiding his touch as she handed him the torch. 'Thanks.'

Safe inside the house, she leaned against the breakfast bar and tried to calm her inner turbulence, struggling to reassert the normal even temperament she took for granted. Hoping it might help, she concentrated on listening for the reassuring sound of the engine starting in Steve's car.

In vain. When the tap came on the door her heart leapt in her breast, and she had to force herself to walk sedately across and open it.

'It's not the solenoid,' Niko told her calmly, eyes

slightly narrowed. 'It's more likely to be the battery, although judging by the state of the engine it could be a multitude of other things. Whatever, it means you've got no way of getting to work tomorrow.'

She'd already worked this out. 'I'll hire a car until I get the battery fixed,' she told him sturdily.

He frowned. 'But how will you get to Waipuna tomorrow morning? Walk?'

The flick of sarcasm in his tone irritated her into retorting, 'Yet another advantage of living in a small town. If I talk sweetly to Ted at the hire firm, he'll bring a car out to me.' If he had any vehicles to spare. Ted ran a very small concern—more a hobby than a business.

In a voice she didn't recognise Niko said, 'A friend of yours, is he?'

'You could call him a friend,' she said, keeping her tone level and distant. It was no business of his. Actually, Ted had been Steve's fishing companion. Of the same age and with similar tastes, they'd spent many days out in Ted's launch.

The telephone's shrill summon startled her.

Niko said, 'Answer it—it's probably the police.'

Sure enough, she recognised the voice that said, 'Elana, it's Phil. Bad news, I'm sorry. Not official, mind you—you'll need to get the car examined by a mechanic for insurance purposes, but it looks to us as though it's a write-off.'

She closed her eyes. 'Oh—*curses*.'

'Yeah. Listen, how are you going to get to work tomorrow?'

'I'll manage.'

'You realise that it might take some time for you to get the insurance pay-out? And you know how much it costs to hire a car?'

In some ways Phil was like an older brother. He clearly had a pretty good idea of her financial situation, and, although she didn't mind that, she did not want to be conducting this conversation with him while Niko watched with a hard blue gaze and an expression on his handsome face that chilled her.

Turning her head away, she said, 'Yes, I do. Thanks for ringing, Phil.'

'Sure, but if you can't get a lift, ring me.'

She smiled. 'Not going to happen, Phil,' and hung up.

'Your policeman schoolmate, I gather,' Niko said ironically.

'Yes.'

'Not good news, I'm guessing.'

'No.' She shrugged, covering a yawn with her hand. 'His considered opinion—and that of the other cop on duty—is that my car's a write-off.'

'I see. What time do you start work?'

'Eight o'clock,' she said automatically, then stared at him. 'Why?'

'I'll give you a lift in.'

'No, that's not necessary,' Elana returned swiftly, adding rather too vehemently, 'I can deal with this.'

He shrugged. 'Are you always this intransigent when you're offered some neighbourly help?'

Suddenly she wanted him gone. Tension overwhelmed her, fuelled by a surge of dangerously volatile sensation, a yearning to yield, to let him take over.

She bit her lip to stem an impetuous flood of words, and took a deep breath. 'I can cope. *I do not need to be rescued.*' She marched across the room and opened the door onto the night, holding it there. 'Thank you for helping me, and for offering a lift. It's very kind of you but I don't—'

'I'll pick you up at seven-thirty.'

'Niko—don't...' Her voice trailed away.

Gaze darkening, he came towards her. Her breath locked in her lungs. She tried for a defiant stare, only to gasp when he reached out and touched her mouth. Her heart jumped in her breast and, mesmerised, captured by the intensity of his gaze, she couldn't move. Beneath the caress her lips shaped a word—his name—but no sound came from them.

This, she thought dazedly, this was what she'd wanted ever since they'd danced together. This was why she'd looked forward to all those computer chats while he was away. Into her mind came a fleeting reminder of her mother's warning, only to be immediately dismissed. She wasn't planning to marry Niko. She wasn't in love with him. So she'd be perfectly safe...

But she whispered again, 'Don't...'

'Don't?' he asked in a deep voice that revealed he was feeling the same powerful urge. 'Don't what?'

'I don't know,' she whispered against that gentle finger.

'You're shivering. Are you cold?'

'No,' she said. Then in a shaky, dazed voice, 'Yes.'

'Let me warm you.'

He waited for her nod before he pulled her into his embrace. His arms around her were like a bulwark against the world, a safe shield against anything. Delicious, overwhelming anticipation stripped away the last of her defences. Some distant part of her brain ordered her to pull away.

She couldn't.

In a harsh voice he said, 'Elana.'

'Yes,' she breathed.

He bent his head and claimed her mouth as though he'd been longing to kiss her for months, for years...for ever.

And then he lifted his head, and released her. Suddenly cold, she shivered again, and immediately he took her in his arms once more, holding her more gently while he scanned her upturned face. 'What is it? Are you afraid?'

'Yes—no—not really,' she muttered, a powerful pulse of sensation—exquisite, demanding—turning her into a halfwit.

Something—amusement?—glimmered in the steel-blue eyes. 'Which?' he asked in a tone she'd never heard before.

Dazed, in thrall to voluptuous desire, Elana said desperately, 'I'm not afraid of you.'

'Good.' He bent his head and kissed her again, his mouth as urgent and hungry as the fierce need that ricocheted through her.

She could stop him, push him away, prove that she wasn't weak enough to surrender to this wild excitement, but a more reckless, hungry part of her longed for more...

So when he lifted his mouth a fraction above hers, and said in a rigidly controlled voice, 'Unless you want this to go further, stop me now,' she was dismayed.

Without thought, she croaked, 'That's not fair.'

His brows lifted and he stepped back. 'It's your decision.'

Deep in Elana something snapped. She'd fought this potent, compelling attraction because Niko reminded her of her father—but love and passion were two different things. And as she didn't—*couldn't*—love him, there could be no danger. Instinct told her that he would be a good lover...

'Elana?' No impatience in his voice, none in his eyes, he waited while she hesitated.

Every cell in her body longed for him, craved the surcease of passion in his arms with an intensity that crashed through common sense and resistance. He didn't expect anything of her but an affair...one that would end when he went back to whatever palatial mansion he lived in. She'd be safe. And oh, she wanted him with such intensity she had to keep her teeth clenched to stop them from chattering.

He took her in his arms again, holding her more gently while he scanned her upturned face.

'Elana?'

Reassured, she breathed, 'Yes.'

CHAPTER SEVEN

AND NIKO KISSED her again.

All caution forgotten, heady recklessness released the response Elana had been fighting since the night of the Centennial Ball. She was overwhelmed by a clamorous need—voluptuous, compelling, demanding—that banished coherent thought. Responding with a passion she'd never experienced before, she relished the hardening of Niko's lean body against her, mindlessly pressing herself as close as she could.

His arms tightened around her, fuelling the heat that blazed inside her, a yearning to be even closer, a longing for more—for *everything*, a hunger for Niko that claimed her completely.

The realisation hit her like a blow. Unconsciously she stiffened, and instantly he loosened his grip while he scanned her upturned face. 'You are afraid,' he accused harshly.

She swallowed to ease a dry throat, flicked her

tongue along dry lips, and managed to croak, 'I told you, I'm not afraid of you.'

As he claimed her lips once more she felt the explosion of need melting her bones, heating her blood in surrender. This time, when he lifted his head, he asked, 'Which door?'

Elana pointed helplessly towards her bedroom then gasped when he lifted her and strode towards it. She hid her face against his neck, inhaling the subtle skin scent of the man she wanted.

From some distant, barely accessible part of her brain, a voice whispered, *Stop. Stop, before it's too late...*

But another, more primal voice answered, *You want him. Take him...*

Niko nudged the door open with his shoulder, took the three steps across to her bed, its blankets thrown back, and stopped. His arms tightened around her, and he lowered her to her feet, sliding her down the hard length of his body. The heat inside her exploded into a conflagration.

As she grabbed his upper arms to steady herself she registered powerful muscles, his potent male strength and something else—a confidence in herself that vetoed turning back.

He gazed down at her with narrowed, intent eyes. 'You're sure?'

She'd never been *more* sure of anything. Suddenly dumb, she nodded.

'How sure?'

No words would come. Surely he could see how she felt? Why did he demand reassurance? Elana reached out and touched his mouth as he'd touched hers, her finger lingering along the length of his lower lip. 'Kiss me,' she managed.

He laughed deep in his throat and pulled her so close nothing but their clothes separated them, his mouth taking hers with such passion that all fear, all caution died.

When he lifted his head she struggled for a little distance. 'What is it?' he asked, his voice rough.

'You must be too hot.' She began to unbutton his shirt, smoothing the fabric back so she could stroke the skin beneath.

'That's—*you*—are just making me hotter.' But he stood there until the last button was free, then shrugged off the shirt.

Elana's breath stopped in her throat. He was magnificent, bronzed skin revealing the taut muscles beneath. Tentatively she reached out and spread her palm against his chest, shivering as the heat of his body reached her.

'Fair's fair,' he said, his voice lazy. And lifted the hem of the T-shirt she'd donned when she'd got up.

Colour flamed through her cheeks, heated her brow, sizzled through every nerve, every cell as he slowly pulled the shirt up. She made an instinctive move to step away, then stopped, fists clenching as she fought for control while he pulled the soft cloth past her head and tossed it over his shoulder.

Elana had to stop herself from covering her taut breasts with her hands, from turning her back. She looked up into his handsome face—more angular, harder, than she'd seen him before.

'You're blushing,' he said softly. 'Are you shy?'

'I'm not—'

The words dried on her tongue when he bent his dark head and kissed the spot where her shoulder met her neck. Her skin tightened at the gentle scrape of his teeth on her skin, and the swift sweep of his tongue. Every sense sharpened fiercely. Sensation zinged from the pit of her stomach—powerful, desperately clamouring for satisfaction, for the exquisite torture of his mouth on her skin again. She shivered in the circle of his arms, yet felt strangely safe.

He straightened. 'Is this the first time—?'

'No,' she managed, her skin fiery.

'You're beautiful,' he said quietly.

Chilled, because she knew she wasn't beautiful, Elana shook her head and tried to pull back. It had to be a shallow compliment, something he'd probably said to each of his lovers—who'd all been stunning, according to Mrs Nixon.

He loosened his arms, frowning down into her face. 'I mean it. Not conventionally, but you move like a dancer and your skin is exquisite and your eyes manage to be both seductive and intelligent. As for your mouth—'

He lowered his head, banishing her momentary loss of confidence with the sheer, unsullied eroticism of his kiss as their tongues duelled.

Elana's heartbeat rocketed, and with it a sensual anticipation. Either he was the best liar she'd ever met, or he really meant it. Whatever, she didn't care. Love didn't enter this. They'd come together as equals. When it was time to part she might miss the rapture he promised, but she wouldn't be shattered by his absence.

There was no mistaking the guttural note in

his voice when he lifted his head. 'Just looking at you makes me want you.'

She believed him. Her breasts felt heavy and languorous, their rosy centres tight and pleading. She forced her voice into an unnatural steadiness. 'It's mutual.'

But he already knew that. Almost angrily, he said, 'But I have no protection.'

Elana dragged in a sharp breath. Wracked by passion, she muttered, 'It's all right. I'm—I'm safe.'

His gaze sharpened. 'Sure?'

'Absolutely.'

He laughed deep in his throat and kissed her again, saying, 'Good. So am I,' against her eager mouth.

Then, releasing her, he undid his belt. As he stepped out of his trousers she tried to control her quickened, sharp breathing. He was—magnificent. Like some ancient Greek god brought to life, she thought, shuddering with need.

And nothing could slow the hungry sweetness of passion that snaked sinuously through her body, setting her aflame.

After swallowing desperately she managed to

mimic his words of a few seconds ago—seconds that had somehow changed her life. 'Fair's fair.'

Elana pushed her elderly jeans down, dragging in a fierce, hungry breath as his gaze followed her hands, his features hardening into a mask of desire.

He waited until she stepped free and then picked her up and laid her gently, carefully, on the sheet.

She closed her eyes as her fingers fumbled with her narrow briefs. His voice came as a shock.

'Here, let me.'

Desire leapt a boundary, intensifying into something she'd never felt previously while he gently removed her last garment and slid onto the bed beside her.

'Open your eyes,' he said almost beneath his breath.

'Why?'

He laughed softly and kissed each eyelid. Against her lips he said, 'So you know who you're making love to.'

'I know.' Her voice was thick and the words came slowly.

'And because I find your eyes infinitely alluring with those tiny sparkles of gold amidst the green.'

Charmed, she lifted her lashes, and met his

gaze, almost wincing as something odd happened to her heart. Heat flooded her skin and she closed her eyes again when he kissed her once more and slid his arm beneath her, holding her against him while he explored her body with his lips and his hand, driving her so wild with an anguished hunger that she couldn't stop the little whimpers that broke through her lips.

And when his mouth found the pleading tip of her breast delight flowed through her at the sensual tug of his lips, his slow, gentle exploration of her body.

Amid the sensuous turmoil, she recognised the alteration in his heartbeat, and rejoiced. Whatever happened afterwards, she would always know that Niko wanted her as recklessly as she wanted him.

Eventually she could no longer bear such erotic torment. She arched against him, stroking, exploring him as he was discovering her. Under her touch his body flexed, muscles coiling, and he slid his hand further down towards the slick, throbbing heat that ached for something she'd never experienced.

When he reached his destination a shuddering groan tore from her throat and she pressed even harder against him, demanding, seeking, so caught up in the carnal magic of his lovemaking that nothing mattered but his touch. Lost in this torrid anticipation, she could no longer think, no longer make excuses, no longer guard what she was doing.

'Now?'

The harsh, driven intensity of his tone boosted her anticipation to unbearable levels. 'Yes.'

It was all she could say. And all he needed to hear. As she arched against him he thrust into her. The jolt of exquisite pleasure shocked her into crying out, and he froze.

'It's all right,' she managed, her voice a mere thread. And when he didn't move, she tightened her arms against his broad back and lifted her face so that he could see it and whispered harshly, 'Please—'

When he still didn't move, she looked up into his hard, angular face, and arched up, pulling him into her, almost sobbing at the intensity of sensation that surged through her.

'Elana,' he said, making a claim she was more than happy to accept.

The passionate delight he summoned from her flung her into a realm of experience completely beyond anything she'd ever imagined, into a sensory rapture where nothing but Niko and she existed, where *nothing* was more important than giving—and taking.

Because as she crested, as fulfilment hurled her into a blazing ecstasy, he followed.

And then he turned and held her against him while their heartbeats slowed together, and Elana realised with bleak foreboding what she'd just done.

Of course she couldn't be in love with him, but the wild ecstasy of their lovemaking had somehow crashed through the barriers she'd set up. Stupidly, she'd put her heart at risk.

An icy chill had her pull away. He let her go and rolled over onto his back, but she knew he was watching her.

'It's all right,' she told him, keeping her voice steady with an effort.

'You're sure?' No warmth in his voice. No emotion at all.

She hated that tone. Loathed it with an intensity that made her shudder.

'You're cold,' he said, and got up from the bed.

Elana hauled up the sheet to cover her nakedness and closed her eyes against him as he dressed, tall and beautifully built, so experienced in making love that he'd taken her to a voluptuous paradise—a paradise so heartbreakingly seductive she'd be crazy to revisit it.

Her eyes flew open as she felt a blanket being spread over her.

Fully dressed, Niko asked, 'Are you all right?'

'Yes, of course,' she said numbly, wishing he'd leave—and longing for him to stay.

'I'll go now. Will you be able to sleep?'

'Yes, of course,' she repeated, with less than her normal assurance. She managed to produce another smile. 'I'm fine. Really.'

To emphasise her control, she reached out and grabbed her light summer dressing gown from its usual position over the back of the chair beside the bed, and without looking at him got into it. 'I'll lock the door after you,' she said, and forced herself to meet his hard gaze without flinching.

Right then she wanted him gone, so she could recover and become the woman she'd always been, not the reckless, foolish one who'd surrendered to such wild ecstasy in his arms.

He nodded, and turned towards the door. Barefooted, more tense than she'd ever been in her life, she paced across the living room in front of him. At the door she turned to face him with head held high, and said, 'Goodnight.'

It sounded like *goodbye*. Niko looked down at her.

Gone was the woman who'd come alive in his arms, under his touch. She'd retreated into herself as though the flimsy dressing gown were a suit of armour. He had to staunch a fever of desire, an instinct to pull her into his arms and banish that calm control, see her again as she had been in his arms, wild and sensual and recklessly passionate.

Cool air rushed in, carrying with it the salt of the sea and the scent of the gardens and the coastal bush. Recalled to some sort of sanity, he asked, 'Before I go, what's happening to your car?'

'Phil will get a tow truck to take it away. I'll contact my insurance company tomorrow morning.'

Assailed once more by that infuriating, baseless irritation, Niko said more curtly than he intended, 'If there's anything I can do, let me know.'

Her head came up and he caught a flash of fire in her eyes as she returned, 'Thank you, but I'll cope.'

Niko took a couple of steps through the door-

way, then turned. Most of the women in his life—
including the mother whose one independent act
had been her impetuous marriage to his father—
relished being looked after, and expected it to
include an existence of pampered indulgence...

Somehow he couldn't see Elana living such a
life. Her independence was an integral part of her.

'It's just part of being a good neighbour,' he said
smoothly, and watched colour heat her cheekbones as her lashes fluttered down a moment,
then lifted.

'I—sorry—' She swallowed. Another pause,
then more steadily, her tone crisp, 'But I am perfectly capable of running my own life.'

A fierce desire gripped Niko, but this time the
strongly sexual hunger was tempered by an emotion he'd never experienced before, a bewildering
urge to make the world safe for her. His muscles
tensed with the instinct to reach out, pull her into
his arms and tell her that from now on nothing
would ever cause her grief.

He had to call on every bit of discipline, of the
control he prided himself on, before he could step
backwards into the safety of the semi-darkness
outside and say levelly, 'That's obvious. Am I
harassing you?'

Startled, she hesitated, then admitted briefly, 'No—not really.'

'Will it be harassment if I ask Patty West to run you into Waipuna tomorrow morning?' he asked, his voice cool. 'I'm sure she'll have supplies to buy at the supermarket.'

She said, 'I guess—' Then smiled wryly. 'That would be all right, and it would be all right if you drove me in too. I just don't like being out-manoeuvred.'

'Nobody,' he told her crisply, 'enjoys that. All right, if your friend can't get a hire car to you tomorrow morning, ring the homestead and either I or Patty will take you in and collect you after work. Goodnight, Elana, and thank you. Sleep well.'

He turned and strode down the path. Shaken, she held the door open to provide light for him as he walked to his car, then closed it behind him with all the firmness she could muster, although her hand trembled as she locked it.

Why on earth had he thanked her? For the sex?

Had he thanked his other lovers, those elegant, famous creatures he'd taken to bed?

And why on earth had she allowed herself to

surrender? When he'd looked at her with that narrowed, unsparing gaze she should have realised how close she was to losing control. Instead, something wild and irresponsible in her had responded with an intensity that now seemed shocking.

Yet even recalling that forbidden hunger made her shiver with remembered ecstasy.

Once the sound of the car engine died away on the cool, sea-scented night air she drew a deep breath and looked around, feeling as though her world had been tipped on its head. At least she could strive for some sort of normality by washing the mugs they'd used for coffee.

She'd been stupid, telling herself she was safe because she didn't love Count Niko Radcliffe. That had been a coward's way of yielding to a hunger she should have scotched when she first felt it.

Whatever sort of man he was, for her he was danger personified.

'Oh, grow up and stop being over-dramatic,' she said aloud. 'He's used to being chased by women—perhaps he was angry that you made it clear you weren't going to—'

She stopped. Going to what? Going to surrender? Going to provide him the sort of interlude he perhaps expected? Going to forget everything her mother had told her about men who wanted to control, not love?

'Stop obsessing about him,' she commanded, washing one of the coffee mugs with so much vigour the handle cracked and fell into her hand. It was her mother's favourite, decorated with painted pansies.

Furious at her carelessness, she stared at it and told herself to think about organising the insurance tomorrow, work out how she was going to get enough money to reroof the house, to think about—think about—oh, think about *anything* other than her magnetic, dangerous, overbearing neighbour.

She might always regret that she'd surrendered to that mindless hunger, but she'd make sure it never happened again.

And quite possibly Niko could be telling himself exactly the same thing...

At the top of the hill that separated Mana Station from Elana's land, Niko stamped on the brakes and stopped the car just over the cattle stop between the stone pillars. Once out he closed the door and stood frowning over the moon-silvered estuary, trying to draw some peace from it. He'd bought Mana Station because a part of him—perhaps inherited from his father, or from the care that the farmers of San Mari took of their land—made him want to bring it back into life.

Something about farming, about caring for land, about producing food for people, satisfied a deep need in him, as it had for his father. In ten years' time Mana Station would be as it should always have been, green and lush, beautiful and productive.

His gaze swept the moonlit slopes of hills that had once been small volcanoes, lingering on the scars of creeks that were already fenced, and would soon be planted with native trees that would eventually help keep the estuary clear of eroded soil.

Why in hell had he lost control tonight? Dammit, what was it about Elana Grange that stripped him of his usual self-discipline? And why had making love with her seemed so...so what?

The only word that came to mind was *transcendental*. Shocked, he took a couple of steps away from the car and dragged in a deep breath. Whatever Elana roused in him went far deeper than ordinary sexual desire. It smashed through his willpower. He'd made the decision to keep his distance—the *right* decision—because he didn't want to hurt her. Admittedly, she'd had previous experience, but the sort of relationships he'd indulged in previously now seemed sordid and almost cynical.

Yet he'd capitulated to a need that almost made him afraid. Even now, at the memory of her ardently passionate response the fierce hunger that should have been sated stirred into life.

And he was gripped by that growing need to make sure she was safe, to protect her from everything that might cause her pain.

CHAPTER EIGHT

ONCE SHE'D SHOWERED away every trace of Niko Radcliffe and remade her bed with fresh sheets, Elana crawled into bed and lay for hours gazing through the darkness at the ceiling, bitterly aware that she was never going to be able to sleep in this bed again without remembering the blissful, impassioned time she'd spent in Niko's arms.

He might be accustomed to one-night stands, but she wasn't.

Eventually she did fall asleep, but she dreamt of him, a weird jumble of scenes, the memory of which made her blush with chagrin the next morning while she got ready for work.

And she had to stop this right now. She had other, more vital things to worry about.

Like ringing Ted and hiring one of his cars.

Only to learn that he had no available vehicles. Fate, it seemed, was determined to force her to rely—at least for the day—on Niko. She set the phone down, then picked up her lipstick and glowered at her reflection in the mirror. Her gaze met a subtly different woman from the one she'd seen there yesterday morning. Somehow her lips were fuller, and her expression held a languorous softness she'd never seen before.

'You're imagining things,' she told her reflection severely. 'Making love—no, *sex*—wouldn't change the way you look! It didn't before.'

But her previous experience with the man she'd once believed she loved bore no resemblance to the wildfire storm of sensation she'd experienced in Niko's arms. There, she'd learned what utter ecstasy could do—summon a kind of rebirth, a rediscovery of herself. He'd set her alight, changed her for ever.

At the memory a primitive excitement stirred inside her.

'Cool it,' she ordered beneath her breath, frowning belligerently before she turned away. 'It's not going to happen again.'

Reluctantly she rang Mana homestead, dreading the thought of being answered by Niko.

Fortunately it was the housekeeper, who said immediately, 'I was just about to ring you. The boss said you'd need a ride into Waipuna and back again this evening. What time do you want to leave?'

Elana told her, then finished with, 'I'm sorry to break into your day—I'm hoping to be able to hire a car tomorrow. Thanks very much.'

Mrs West laughed. 'No problem, and you'd better thank Niko.'

Her mood a bit lighter, Elana hung up.

Although glad that neither of the two men who'd stolen her car had been badly hurt, she couldn't help vengefully wishing she could have ten minutes alone with them. It wasn't going to happen, so she had to get Steve's car on the road again. She rang the mechanic, who said he'd be there about five-thirty that afternoon.

'That's fine; I'll be home by then.'

He went over the engine carefully, then straightened up and slammed down the bonnet.

Shaking his head, he told her not unsympathetically, 'Quite frankly, Elana, this heap of rust isn't worth fixing. I'm not even going to try. It will never be roadworthy—and money spent on it would buy you a decent second-hand car. Your best bet is to get the scrap-metal guy to take it away.'

She hesitated before asking, 'Have you had a chance to look at *my* own car? Phil told me it's at your workshop.'

'Yes. It's salvageable.'

Relief flooded through her. 'When do you think it will be ready?'

He shrugged. 'Can't give you a definite date. It's an insurance job so it will take at least several days, possibly more than a week.'

Elana winced, but thanked him and waved him goodbye before ringing Ted at the hire company. To her relief, he'd found a car she could hire for the next couple of days.

'But probably only for a few days,' he warned. 'Things are getting busy right now—school holidays, you know.'

Spirits lifting slightly, she thanked him, hung up and slathered her arms and legs and nose with sunscreen lotion before going outside to weed the vegetable garden.

Hiring a car for any length of time would eat into her savings and right then, with the roof needing attention, she didn't need that.

It would be so simple—so economical—so *sensible* to accept Niko's offer.

Sighing, she noticed that snails had done vicious damage to the lettuce plants she'd put in several weeks ago. On her way to the garden shed to pick up slug bait, she stopped when she heard a car coming down the drive. Niko's large four-wheel-drive vehicle turned the corner.

Blood pounded in her ears as though she'd been running a marathon. The tension gripping her was intensified by the caressing breeze that whispered across her bare arms and legs. Regretting the elderly pair of denim shorts she should have thrown out a couple of years ago, and a faded, even older T-shirt in a colour that didn't suit her, she waited and tried to regulate her breathing.

The big vehicle slowed to a halt in the turning circle. Niko got out and her heart twisted. It took a real effort of will to summon a casual, neighbourly smile.

One glance told her this was not the tenderly passionate lover of the previous night. She braced herself as he got out, and said in her most cheerful tone, 'Hello.'

It sounded false. And lame. And stupid.

He narrowed his eyes and demanded, 'What's the matter?'

'Nothing,' she said automatically.

He stopped—too close—and subjected her to an unsparing scrutiny. 'Liar.'

When Elana stiffened, he said, 'Tell me what's worrying you.'

'Why?' And immediately regretted it. How did he reduce her to a defiant teenager?

'Because I might be able to help.'

Now he sounded like that teenager's out-of-patience parent. When Elana hesitated, he went on coolly, 'Independence is all very well, but refusing help is cutting off your nose to spite your face.'

She drew in a sharp breath and looked up. Drat the man, he was smiling! Something odd—a fiercely exultant twist of sensation—quickened her heart, weakened her knees, and throbbed deep inside her, summoning needs she needed to ignore.

In her best brisk, no-nonsense tone, she said, 'If you must know, I've just found out that Steve's car is not a viable proposition.' She looked up and finished in a voice she tried to keep unconcerned, 'Not worth fixing.'

He frowned. 'So how are you planning to deal with that?'

'I've just been speaking to Ted, and he's managed to organise a car for me for the rest of the week.' She added with a smile that held more wryness than humour, 'And the wreckers will take Steve's old jalopy away.' She added, 'I don't seem to be having much luck with vehicles, but I'm hoping it's just a passing phase.'

And was startled when Niko laughed in genuine amusement. It changed his face entirely. Not exactly softening it—his features were too strong and striking for that—but the warmth increased his powerful male magnetism.

So much so that she found herself almost shivering in the sunlight. *Go back to being the domineering man you really are,* she told him silently.

Like this, he was altogether too much, and her foolish, impressionable heart was softening, melting...

'A passing phase? I imagine everyone you know is hoping that too,' he told her, still smiling. 'Mrs Nixon, for one.'

Elana relaxed a little, but asked suspiciously, 'Have you been talking to her?'

'She's been talking to me,' he told her.

She frowned. 'She's a dear, but she worries too much about me.'

'Possibly she feels that someone has to worry about you.'

'It's not necessary,' she told him.

Her distant tone should have warned him off but he said, 'She told me you have no family.'

Frown deepening, she shrugged. 'Well, none that I know of. My mother grew up in care, and Steve was English. He never said anything about a family.'

'What about your birth father?'

A few seconds of silence preceded her abrupt answer. 'As far as I know, none.' This time, her tone was definitely aloof.

Hard eyes hooded, Niko said, 'It's just as well you have Mrs Nixon, then. I've just had a call from the Prime Minister's office; I have a meeting with him in Wellington. After that I'm flying to the Maldives.'

The Maldives? Meeting someone there, perhaps? Someone gorgeous and blonde from his world...?

A fierce pang that sharpened into an agonising jealousy hit Elana, scrambling her brain.

Was he running away? One glance at his face told her she was being stupid. His inbred arrogance would prevent that. Controlling a stab of pain, she said lightly, 'Have fun.'

The throbbing sound of a helicopter's engines broke into the calm air. He said, 'That's my chopper. Will you drive me back to Mana?'

The question was delivered in a tone that made it sound like an order. She asked, 'Why?' her voice so nakedly bewildered she hastened to add, 'Why is that necessary? Are you all right?'

His smile was brief and mirthless. 'I'm fine, but I'm lending you this car while I'm away.'

'No,' she said automatically. Was this some kind of payoff for making love with him?

Surely not...

'Yes.' He spoke calmly, blue gaze level and hard. 'I want to make sure you can drive it properly. It's bigger than the cars you're accustomed to.'

Mortified, Elana had to stop herself from wringing her hands. It took all of her self-control to say, 'Why are you doing this?'

Broad shoulders lifting in a shrug, he said dryly, 'I won't be needing it while I'm away.'

Which sounded as though he was going to be gone for some time. She took a deep breath and tried to sound logical and level-headed. 'Niko, this is taking neighbourliness to extremes, and it's not necessary. Thank you,' she added belatedly, her voice trailing away as he tossed the keys to her. Instinctively she caught them, clutching them as he turned away and strode towards the road.

'What on earth are you doing?' she demanded.

'Walking back to Mana,' he said over his shoulder.

She said uncertainly, 'You're—this is ridiculous.'

And prickled at another of those dismissive shrugs.

'Sensible,' he said laconically. 'It doesn't pay to keep politicians waiting when you want something from them. And as you told me not so long ago, it's not very far to Mana from here.'

Torn between anger with him for putting her in this position, and chagrin at the sense of loss that ached through her, Elana glowered at his back. Then she took a deep breath, and surrendered.

After all, once she'd hired a car she wouldn't need to use this one...

'Oh, all right,' she said churlishly. 'Get in, and I'll drive you back.'

If he's smiling when he turns around, he can jolly well walk.

But the threat vanished when he turned. He wasn't smiling. Instead he looked his usual self—totally composed, formidably compelling, and enigmatic.

As though nothing had happened between them.

Niko hid a wry smile as he got into the car. Where had she got that fierce independence? And why on earth did he want to protect her from everything that could upset her, when she was so clearly bent on resisting him?

Until last night. He'd had no intention of making love with her. Yet when she'd looked at him, and touched him, some hidden need he'd never experienced before had made surrender inevitable.

And it had been like nothing before, sweet and fiery and intoxicating.

But going nowhere. Elana's attitude made that more than obvious. So he'd put her from his mind and concentrate on the business ahead, and soon he'd be able to view the situation without this lingering need.

Elana climbed behind the wheel of the vehicle and set her mind to driving it. Fortunately Niko was helpful. Her tension gradually relaxed into something like confidence as they neared the homestead.

'You're a good driver,' he told her as she slowed down. 'I've contacted the police and my insurance company and told them you'll be driving this until you get your own car back.'

She bit back a request to let her know how long he'd be away. One night's passionate lovemaking didn't give her any rights at all.

Besides, he might have every intention of staying away.

Ignoring the acute twinge of anguish caused by that possibility, she eased the vehicle to a stop outside the homestead, and without switching off the engine said, 'Thank you. Travel safely.'

He got out and came around to the driver's door. 'Try to keep out of trouble.'

Elana managed a smile. 'I think you must be a bad omen for me. Trouble arrived with you.'

His expression hardened. 'Rubbish.' He reached in and switched off the engine, holding the key in his hand as she gaped at him.

'Before I leave,' he said, 'I want to ask you something. Do you recognise the calls a kiwi makes?'

Bewildered, she said, 'Yes, I do. I hear them calling sometimes at night. Why?'

'I noticed a dead one on the side of the road last night—obviously run over. The person I spoke to at the Department of Conservation office said it's not uncommon, and asked if I'd noticed signs of them on Mana.'

Even more surprised, she asked, 'Have you?'

'No.'

'On the road they get dazzled by headlights. On farms, dogs are powerfully attracted to them. It's apparently hard to convince some people that their nice, friendly spaniel or obedient cattle dog will happily kill New Zealand's iconic bird. And until they're almost mature they're unable to protect themselves from stoats.'

He nodded. 'So the DOC ranger told me. I'm considering setting up a kiwi protection zone on the peninsula. Would you be interested in coming on board?'

Her first instinct was to say no. It would mean she saw even more of him, and she didn't dare. But native birds all around New Zealand were in danger from introduced predators. This was a new aspect of Niko, one she admired. After several seconds, she said, 'Yes.'

And wondered bleakly if she'd just made a very bad mistake.

'You know the other landowners here better than I do. What do you think of the possibility of them joining in?'

Frowning, Elana swiftly assessed their neighbours. 'I think they probably would. It's worth a try.'

'Indeed,' he agreed, and glanced at his watch, then held out the car key. 'I'd better be on my way.'

'I—yes. Thank you.'

His brief smile held no humour. 'Elana, it's all right,' he said calmly. 'I can see you're suffering post-coital remorse, but I don't think the less of you, if that's what—'

'I'm not! It's not that big a deal,' she said desperately, hugely embarrassed. Because his opinion of her mattered far too much.

His raised brows brought swift colour to her skin. 'Oh, darn,' she muttered. 'That sounded awful. I can cope with borrowing your car, but you don't have to feel in any way responsible for me, just because we—well—because we...' Her voice died away and she was blushing like some adolescent after her first grown-up kiss. 'Because we made love,' she blurted.

He gave her an ironic look. 'Was it so hard to say?'

Unable to come up with any answer, Elana bit her lip, and was enormously relieved when he said, 'I'm sorry, that was crass of me. I'll see you again in about a fortnight.'

'Bon voyage,' she managed.

He nodded and turned and walked away.

Blinking, she set her jaw and set the car in motion, concentrating fiercely as she drove it towards Waipuna.

Was this some sort of kiss-off—*Goodbye, thanks for the sex, now forget about it?*

For Niko, had last night just been another episode in a series of one-night stands?

No! Horrified by the fierce pang of desolation that shot through her, she drew in a shaking breath. He had taken her, made her so completely his that she was no longer the woman she'd been before. Fiercely tender, he'd claimed her as though he'd been searching for her all his life and found her at last.

Don't read so much into it, she warned herself. *You're fantasising...*

The following morning she woke to an email from him, informing her that if she needed any help, she was to email him. And he'd contact her in two days at ten a.m. NZ time on the computer using the VOIP tool. Signed, Niko.

Cold, brief and chillingly matter-of-fact.

Well, what had she expected? It was completely stupid to suffer that aching hollowness of loss again, as though he'd meant anything more to her than a casual fling.

Casual? Wrong word.

Very wrong word. A kind of panic gripped her, an ominous understanding that last night had somehow changed her. But—judging by the tone of his farewell, if farewell it could be called—it had had no effect on him.

She should be relieved.

But why did every impersonal word in that email feel like a stab to the heart?

Stop thinking of him. At least she still had the Mana project to keep her busy. Apart from the considerable sum she was being paid for doing it, it would help keep her mind off Niko, and her humiliatingly fervent desire to trust him.

Gritting her teeth, she called the station. She needed to organise a routine that suited them all while Niko was away. 'Or I could bring the documents back home,' she suggested, unwilling to be reminded of Niko every day she went to the homestead.

David West was silent for a moment before saying, 'I don't think the boss would agree to that. They're pretty fragile.'

Bother! After she'd hung up she walked out onto the deck to survey the estuary, narrowing her eyes against the shimmer of early summer sunlight across the water, the wash of gold highlighting the hills on the other side of the water. Each Christmas, the silver buds on the ancient pohutukawa trees burst open into pompons of scarlet and crimson and russet, a vivid contrast to the deep green leaves.

Would Niko be here then?

So much had happened recently...her mother's death, Jordan's accident, the theft of her car, the discovery of the documents...

And meeting Niko Radcliffe.

Relieved by the imperative summons of the telephone, she ran inside. It was the roofer, who gave her a date for his arrival. She hung up, glad yet worried. Even with the income she was earn-

ing from her work at Mana, she'd have to stick
to a pretty strict budget for the next few months.

Bracingly she told herself she'd coped with everything else, so she'd cope with this, as well as
with her stupid heart's yearning after a man she
didn't dare allow herself to trust.

As the days slid by she became more and more
interested in the documents, especially the diaries. She read accounts of accidents, fatalities,
parties and weddings and balls, comments on the
news of the day, and one day discovered what she
suspected to be a faded bunch of love letters tied
up with a blue satin ribbon.

Because it seemed rude to even consider un-
tying that bow to read the outpourings of someone's heart, she put them untouched to one side.
Niko was due to contact her in another couple of
days, so she'd mention them to him.

And try to rid herself of her desperate, embarrassing anticipation at the thought of seeing him
on screen again. Memories of his lovemaking—
passionate and tender—vied with memories of his
coolness afterwards. Yet the last time he'd contacted her, he seemed—different, more relaxed,
as though he enjoyed talking to her.

A knock on the door broke into her thoughts.

David West, the manager, apologised for interrupting and said, 'The kids from the high school will arrive here shortly to do some more tree planting. They might get here before I get back from picking the boss up from the airport, but they won't bother you, they know where to go.' He smiled at her startled face.

Niko helping children plant trees? Previously she'd have found it difficult to imagine Niko with a group of young adolescents, but those impassioned minutes in his arms had shown her a different side of him...a side she could trust?

Almost, she thought uncertainly.

David West smiled. 'He's very good with them—treats them like adults, but makes sure they don't get carried away with fooling around. They think he's great. On the first day they came one of the boys was acting the goat, and Niko put a stop to it straight away. Did me good to see the kid settle down to work. Hasn't blotted his copybook since.' As he turned to go, he said, 'By the way, if you're wondering where Patty is, she's at the dentist's—toothache hit her in the middle of the night. Can you take the phone calls if there are any? Just take a message.'

'Yes, of course.'

Elana went back to her office. She'd felt she was learning to understand Niko Radcliffe, but almost every day she learned something about him that turned her preconceptions upside down. Slowly, carefully—almost reluctantly—she was learning to trust him.

Only last night, at dinner with the Nixons, she'd been told of his large donation to the retirement home in Waipuna, and his stipulation that the amount not be circulated. 'He's already making a big difference to Waipuna,' Mrs Nixon had observed, 'and not just financially.'

An hour later, when the telephone summoned her, Elana picked up the receiver and said briskly, 'Mana Station.'

The caller was a woman with a very English accent, clipped and abrupt, who said, 'I want to speak to Niko Radcliffe.'

Startled, Elana told her, 'I'm sorry, he's not here. Can I take a message?'

'No. Who are you? His secretary?'

No reason for her to be so rude. 'No.'

'Oh, his latest girlfriend, I suppose.' Her tone altered. 'If that's so, then take care. He's a brute—and not just verbally. Watch out for his fists if you make him angry.'

Stunned, Elana opened her mouth to speak, but it was too late. The connection had been cut off.

Feeling sick, she put down the receiver and got rather shakily to her feet. A chill iced her stomach and tightened her skin. Shivering, she walked over to the open window and stared unseeingly out.

Who on earth had that been?

She wasn't ever likely to know. A woman who knew Niko well, apparently.

And who seemed to have good reason to hate him. She'd spoken with real venom, spitting out the words as though they were weapons.

Elana took in a great lungful of warm, sea-scented air, and turned away. Questions—hateful questions with no answers—buzzed like wasps through her brain. She winced, feeling as though something rare and precious had been shattered into painful splinters. She'd even allowed herself to believe she could trust him...

Her nausea intensified into pain, so all-encompassing it overcame any physical agony she'd ever experienced. Not again, she thought wearily. In a world with plenty of decent men, was she doomed to run across only those who were abusers?

First her father, who'd beaten her mother, and

then Roland, who'd resented anything that took her attention away from him—but mostly her work and her affection for her mother and step-father and friends.

At least she'd realised what was happening and managed to break their relationship off without bearing too many emotional scars.

She simply couldn't imagine Niko striking a woman.

But then, she'd noticed no warning signs when she'd fallen in love with Roland, either. It had taken her several months to realise that his constant criticism, his demands that she always tell him where she was and whatever she was planning to do, the days of frigid silence when he thought she'd disobeyed him, were all a form of abuse that was stripping her of confidence.

Emotional manipulation was bad enough; physical abuse had to be worse. Love was a much more complicated affair than the basic physical urge to mate. It involved friendship—and trust.

Perhaps, she thought bleakly, she was a very slow learner.

Had it amused Niko to take her to bed? Had she just been a convenient focus for a temporary lust?

He certainly hadn't wasted any time in heading off overseas. It seemed more and more likely.

Yet even with the shock of that call numbing her brain, heat from the memory of their passion stirred deep within her body.

She didn't really know Niko at all, so she couldn't—dared not—trust him. Therefore she couldn't be in love with him. Yet a primal sense of loss that had no basis in common sense ached through her.

And wailing about it wasn't going to solve anything. So she'd just make sure she never surrendered to her baser urges again.

In the meantime, she had work to do. She sat down at the desk and tried to absorb the description of preparations for a late Victorian garden party held in the gardens of the homestead, as told by the eighteen-year-old daughter of the house.

Until she was interrupted by a voice behind her, deep and dark and cool, and instantly recognisable. 'That must be a fascinating read.'

Her heart leapt and her fingers froze on the keyboard.

She'd been dreading this moment. She slowly turned, bracing herself against a swift, heartfelt delight that terrified her.

'No,' she said, adding foolishly, 'I didn't hear the helicopter.'

'It's having an overhaul. Dave met me at the airport.' Brows almost meeting over ice-blue eyes, Niko demanded, 'What's the matter? You look as though you've seen a ghost.'

'Nothing,' she said automatically.

Thoughts jostled through her brain, none of them making much sense.

She swallowed and babbled, 'I wasn't expecting you. I thought you said you were going to be away for a fortnight, but it's only been a week.' And stopped, mortified, because now he'd know she'd been counting them. Hastily she added, 'I heard the car, but I thought it was Mrs West coming back from the dentist.' *Tell him now, get it over.* 'Someone rang for you a while ago.'

Oh, she was making a total pig's breakfast of this! His brows shot up, and she finished rapidly, 'Judging by her accent she's English. She didn't leave a message.'

Alarmed, she found herself scanning his face, searching, she realised, for some clue as to whether he'd been expecting the call.

His expression gave nothing away. 'If it's important whoever it was will contact me again,' he said indifferently. And came across to look at the old book opened before her on the desk. 'What is this?'

Every sense sharpening, she had to swallow before she could tell him. She prayed for him to leave so she didn't have to endure the faint scent of his skin—musky and very male, something she recalled only too vividly from their lovemaking.

'It's fascinating,' she ended staunchly. 'I'm so glad these documents have been saved. I wonder what the people you bought Mana from would have done with them if they'd known of their existence. Burnt them, probably.'

Niko straightened, looking down at her with slightly narrowed eyes. 'Obviously you didn't like them.'

She shrugged and turned back to the diary, hoping he'd go away. 'I didn't know them. Nobody did. They lived in Auckland, and spent much of the time overseas. The owner was no farmer. He just saw Mana as an investment that he could plunder.'

'Is that how you think I consider it?'

Without needing to think, she shook her head. 'No. I've seen the changes you've made here—the paddocks already look much greener and the fences are in good shape again. And nobody who sees the place as a cash cow would have brought the homestead back to life, or be paying me for transcribing all these documents before they crumble into dust.' She paused, then added, 'Or have organised a group of schoolchildren to come and plant trees to stop sedimentation in the estuary.'

'Yet I detect a certain amount of constraint in your tone,' he observed dryly. 'Why?'

Go away, Elana urged silently.

His nearness affected her like a physical touch, her skin tightening as sensation ran wild through her, quickening her pulse and shortening her breath.

Again she swallowed. 'Sacking Mr Percy was—unfortunate.'

'How did you know he was sacked?'

'His wife told—' Too late, she stopped.

His smile held no humour. 'She told Mrs Nixon,' he finished for her. 'And Mrs Nixon told you.'

'Yes. She knows I can be trusted not to tell anyone else.'

His gaze hardened. 'I'll tell you why he is no longer working here. The previous owner wasn't the only person siphoning money from Mana. The manager did his share of that too.'

Stunned, Elana couldn't think of a word to say. He went on, 'His wife doesn't know about it, and I have no intention of telling her. But I certainly couldn't trust him.'

'No,' she said numbly. 'No, of course not.'

To her immense relief he stepped back.

'I'll leave you to your work,' he said. 'I hope you'll have lunch with me.'

She hesitated, then swivelled around. 'Patty's been to the dentist, she might not feel up to making lunch for you. If that's so, I'll do it.'

His smile was tinged with irony. 'I'm quite capable of making my own, but thank you. We'll eat together out on the veranda.'

And he walked out of the room, draining it—and Elana—of energy. At the click of the closing door she sagged and drew in a long, softly shuddering breath while a mixture of barely controllable emotions fought for supremacy. Mingled with the aftermath of her shock at seeing him again so unexpectedly was pain for lost trust—and a fierce joy that still shocked her.

Had he taken her complete surrender as a signal that their passionate relationship would continue whenever he was at Mana? It didn't seem likely. There had certainly been no sign of desire in his voice, in his expression...

Elana told herself she was glad. She *had* to be glad his emotions hadn't been touched by their lovemaking.

But those maddened hours spent in his arms had fundamentally changed her in some way she didn't feel ready to examine. His tenderness had touched her deeply, bringing with it trust—a trust totally shattered by the telephone call. As well as anger in that unknown voice there had been a note of yearning, as though its owner was still trapped by longing.

That memory would keep her safe, Elana vowed.

After all, Niko wasn't going to be at Mana often, or for long. He had the world at his feet, and several empires to rule...

At midday she got up, picked up her bag with her lunch in it, and headed for the door. She had no idea which veranda he'd be eating on, but she walked to the one she'd been to before, and sure enough, there was a table set for two overlooking the estuary, and Mrs West bustling out into the sunshine with a tray.

Catching sight of Elana, she said, 'Ah, there you are. I thought I might have to knock and let you know the time.'

Elana forced a smile. 'My stomach's better than any clock. How did your appointment with the dentist go?'

'Remarkably well. And really, visiting the dentist nowadays is nothing like it used to be, thank heavens.' She set the tray on the table and smiled past Elana. 'Hello, Niko. Welcome back.'

Elana had to stop herself from clenching a hand across her breast to hide the jumping of her heart. He'd changed clothes, but, even clad in jeans and a casual shirt that revealed the strength of muscular arms, he was still the sophisticated tycoon.

And in spite of the fear that drove her decision not to resume any sort of relationship with him but the most distant, some primitive, unregenerate part of her was deeply, shamelessly glad she'd chosen to greet the summer day by wearing a dress in the soft amber that suited her so well.

The housekeeper gone, Niko said, 'I hope you've got sunscreen on. Five minutes in this sun will probably be enough to burn that creamy skin of yours. I'll move the table into the shade.'

Something in his tone and the swift survey that accompanied it made her acutely conscious of bare arms and a scooped neckline. Her dress was far from revealing, yet her skin was swept by heat. Every time she thought of him, memories intruded, memories she knew she'd never be able to banish.

Thank heavens she'd picked up that phone... If she hadn't, she might be allowing herself to surrender to his overwhelming charisma. Even knowing what sort of man he was, she had to guard against the heady clamour of awareness.

Trying for a brisk, no-nonsense tone, she replied, 'Don't worry. At this time of the year I don't step outside without slathering myself in sunscreen.'

For Niko Mrs West produced a splendid and substantial lunch of fish on a salad of roasted tomatoes. As she opened her lunchbox, Elana wished she'd made easy-to-eat sandwiches instead of a somewhat unwieldy wrap filled with the leftovers of her previous night's dinner.

Normally she enjoyed sitting on the beautifully restored Victorian veranda fringed by white-painted wooden lace around the guttering, while waves hushed gently on the beach through the trees, and seagulls swooped and called and landed on the lawn, watching them with bright eyes as they ate.

But since she had made love—no, no, *had sex*—with Niko, nothing seemed normal.

'If you're going to make a habit of having lunch out here you'll have to post a sign saying *Please do not feed the gulls*,' she observed, hoping her voice showed no signs of her inner turmoil.

He smiled. 'That's a possibility. I enjoy eating al fresco. I noticed you have a table on your terrace, so I presume you do too. Do you find the gulls a nuisance?'

'Sometimes.' It was stupid to allow herself to be so affected by him, but the memories of her temporary madness had her on a knife-edge.

How on earth did people deal with this sort of situation?

With calmness and common sense and willpower. And conversation, no matter how banal. She said, 'There's a description in one of the diaries of the wedding of one of the sons. They were married in Waipuna, but the reception was held out here, and was clearly a huge event.'

'You sound as though you're enjoying delving into their past.'

'I am.'

Relieved to steer the conversation away from personal subjects, she said, 'I didn't know that you have schoolchildren planting trees for you.'

He shrugged. 'The school has a very vigorous eco group. I heard about it, and wondered if they might be interested in helping to plant the creek banks to stop sedimentation of the estuary. When I contacted the school the headmaster put it to the parents and the group, who all agreed it was a good idea. One afternoon a month they come out and do some work.'

'Are you planning to go ahead with a kiwi conservation group?'

'Yes,' he said calmly. 'Interested?'

She hesitated, then said, 'Yes.' And added, 'I don't know much about other similar groups in Northland, but it's going to take quite a bit of organising.' And had to stop herself from offering to help with that. Stumbling a little, she went on, 'Trapping predators is a big part of it.'

'I know that. You sound surprised.'

'I suppose I am,' she admitted.

He shrugged. 'I remember my father telling me

of the discovery of the last living takehe not very far from where we lived. Until then they'd been believed to be extinct.'

Impressed, Elana nodded. Years previously, New Zealanders had been delighted and astounded when the tiny group of birds had been discovered. Since then, there had been a successful effort to raise the numbers.

Niko said, 'I see you know about them.'

'I've read about them. One day I hope to actually see some.'

'Our ancestors didn't understand the damage they were doing to New Zealand's unique wildlife when they chopped down so much of the native forest and turned it into farms.' And with an abrupt change of subject, 'What do you think should be done with all these documents once you've finished with them?'

'The local museum would love them,' she told him, 'but it's run by volunteers, and these documents really should be in some place where they can be cared for properly.'

He nodded. 'Once they are digitised the museum can have copies. The earliest records of my father's station were burnt in a fire that destroyed the original homestead some time in the middle of last century.'

'Oh, that's such a pity.'

His smile held a certain amount of irony, yet it warmed her. 'There speaks the historian. I'm sure the original owners of this station would agree with you.'

'I don't know of any other repository like this in Northland. Everything's in surprisingly good condition.'

Later she'd ask herself grimly what magic he'd produced to talk her into researching a safe place to donate them to. Not that he'd had to try very hard—after working with the documents she took an almost proprietorial interest in them.

She was relieved when Mrs West came out with a tray. 'Coffee and tea,' she announced cheerfully, setting it down on the table. 'If you're too hot, I'll bring out a cold drink.'

Niko looked down at Elana, something in his gaze kindling flames inside her. 'Tea, I presume?' he said levelly.

Her initial tension had been smoothed over by a perilous sense of companionship, but it took an effort to give him what she hoped was a cheerful smile. 'Yes, thank you.'

He chose coffee, and once the housekeeper had left began to pour it. Elana watched his lean hands—hands that had given her such exquisite delight—manipulate the coffee pot. Once again she was caught up in a strange, poignant flash of *déjà vu*, as though she should recognise this garden, this house—this man.

As though they were hugely important to her...

Her hands shook. Hoping he hadn't noticed, she took a deep breath, and pretended to look around the garden. Although it was familiar now, she was suddenly filled by an enormous contentment, as though she had come home.

The sunlight sending down a summer benediction onto the tangled growth in what had once been carefully planted beds, the hum of bees foraging in a regiment of lilies below the veranda railings, the estuary flashing blue between the heavy swooping branches of pohutukawa trees— all reminded her of Sleeping Beauty's castle garden in her book of fairy tales. The conversation she'd had with Niko on that was still sharply etched in her brain.

She stole a glance across the table, her cheeks heating when she met Niko's half-closed eyes.

Deep inside her, an odd sweet burn of sensation tightened, insistent, demanding.

'Drink your tea,' Niko said, his voice harsh. 'Then I'll take you home.'

Almost she nodded. Just in time, she squelched the urge. She knew instantly what would happen once they got home. Her body craved what he was offering, yearned for it, longed to surrender to the promise in his eyes. And her foolish mind wanted it too—wanted him with a hunger that threatened to overwhelm any weak vestige of common sense, ignore the voice inside her that reminded her she could not trust this man.

She was afraid to trust him—but even more afraid of trusting herself.

Her throat dried, but she managed to say, 'I'm working right now.'

'I think I can arrange to change that.'

Her gaze snared by his, she managed to hold his gaze and shake her head. Twice. 'No.'

CHAPTER NINE

IT WAS MORE a croak than a word, but Niko understood.

Almost certainly, judging by Elana's set shoulders and the defiant lift of her chin, she meant, 'Not again, not ever...'

The fierce anger that gripped him shocked him into silence as he fought for control. What followed was even more disturbing—an emotion so strong it almost overwhelmed him. Dismay? No, infinitely more than that.

He drew in a hard breath and told himself sardonically that he'd fallen into the classic playboy's trap of assuming that money and power would buy him any woman.

Not this one.

A strange kind of relief took him totally by surprise. Another quality to discover in this intriguing, maddening woman—she would not be bought.

After a swift glance that took in the harsh contours of his face, the thin line of his mouth and his hooded eyes, Elana braced herself for his response—anger, scorn, contempt.

But when he spoke his voice was level and without inflexion. 'I notice you've been using the car.'

'Only to come down here when it's wet,' she told him. Like his, her voice lacked colour and expression. 'The wife of one of your workers has found a job in Waipuna, so I go with her on the days I work at the shop. I pay for some of her petrol costs. It's working very well.'

'Feel free to call on me if you need transport,' Niko told her crisply.

'That's very kind of you,' she returned, vowing never to do so.

The rest of the conversation was conducted with impersonal politeness. He showed her the plans drawn up by the landscape architect he'd hired to return the homestead grounds to their former glory. After scanning them, she told him she was glad that he'd insisted on staying close to the Victorian concept of the garden.

Finally back in her office, she could allow herself to collapse into the chair in front of the computer and endeavour to assemble her thoughts into some sort of coherence.

Only to fail entirely. Resisting Niko had taken enormous self-control; every cell in her body had demanded a renewal of the sexual delight she knew he could give her. However, she'd done it and now he understood she wasn't in the market for an affair, she could relax. She was safe.

But she didn't feel safe. She felt desolate. He hadn't told her why he'd returned early, but his cool attitude made it obvious that whatever he felt for her meant little to him.

Her worlds and Niko's had touched, but there could be no connection between a man with a pedigree a mile long who could probably buy any small country he fancied, and a woman working in a tiny town in New Zealand, with a bank account that was practically non-existent until the insurance money for her car was paid into it. At least work had started on the roof thanks to her job at Mana Station, although she still needed a loan to pay off the balance.

And with any luck, Niko would soon leave Mana and head off to an exotic place where beautiful women in designer bikinis would appreciate him far more than she dared.

The sooner the better.

It took concentrated effort to make any progress with the document she was working on, but eventually the time came for her to pack up and go home.

But it was with a knot of something too close to apprehension in her stomach that she switched off the computer and left the room—a sensation that intensified a hundredfold when she went outside. Niko was standing by the car, and as she walked towards him he delivered one of those unsmiling, ice-blue assessments.

Like checking out a car he wanted to buy, she thought, stiffening with resentment.

Niko watched her, wondering how the hell she created such havoc in him. One word from her, delivered with brutal succinctness, had made it quite clear she didn't want to further their relationship—if several hours in bed together could be called a relationship.

Of course it wasn't. It had been an interlude, nothing more, and he'd soon get over this—this unruly clamour of emotions. He glanced at his watch and said coolly, 'I owe you five minutes' overtime.'

She shrugged. 'No, you don't. It took me that to get here from my—*the*—office. It's a huge house.'

'The Victorians usually assumed they were going to have huge families,' he returned, and opened the door for her.

Watching her climb gracefully into the vehicle stirred something intensely potent within him.

Dammit, he wanted her, foolishly, crazily. But she didn't want him.

Regret? Possibly. But she hadn't been a virgin. And in his arms she'd become a creature of fire and spirit, a wild and blazing sensualist.

Stop that line of thought right now, he thought uncompromisingly.

It could be another man, of course. Possibly her policeman friend—who might, or might not, be married.

Chagrined by the flash of fierce resentment that caused, he closed the door behind her before walking around the vehicle. Out of sight, he stopped a moment, fixing his gaze on the house, now as pristine as when it was built over a century ago, before surveying the garden, still to be rescued and restored.

He hadn't been able to prise Elana from his mind while he'd been away, and he'd been looking forward to seeing her again. Dammit, he was in danger of making an idiot of himself over her.

It's called rejection, he thought sardonically, *and it's not the first time it's happened to you.*

As a callow youth he'd had his heart dented a couple of times, but he'd learned to deal with it. His ego was suffering—no, it was far more than just his ego—but whatever had caused Elana to draw back was her business, not his.

Although he needed to make sure of one thing.

As he drove through the stone entrance to Mana, he asked, 'Are you quite sure you're not pregnant?'

He sensed her stiffening beside him. After a moment she said frigidly, 'One hundred per cent positive.'

'Good,' he said, and left it at that.

Silence stretched tautly between them until they'd reached the small building she called home. Without looking at him, one hand on the door handle, she said steadily, 'Thank you for the loan of your car, but I don't need it now. It's a very pleasant walk to Mana as well as being good exercise for me.'

Niko controlled his swift response, a mixture of frustration and anger. 'If it's raining someone will collect you and bring you home.'

Eyes darkening, she frowned at him, then

opened the door and climbed out. 'That won't be necessary. I do have rain gear that I can use.'

It took all of Niko's self-control not to grit his teeth. However, one glance at her standing beside the vehicle, shoulders square, her lush mouth tight and her gaze level and inflexible, convinced him that getting out of the car to tell her she was being foolishly stubborn was not going to make any difference to her decision.

She said, 'Thank you for the offer, though. And the ride home.'

He replied laconically, 'My pleasure,' and put the car in motion, leaving with a wave of his hand through the open window.

Torn anew by conflicting emotions, Elana fought back a regret that threatened to drown her, and turned to go into the house. It should have welcomed her like the refuge it had always been, but it felt alien, lonely, bereft of memories...

No, not bereft. One memory was engraved on her brain, into her skin, in every cell of her body. Whenever she walked inside she'd remember Niko's passionate lovemaking—the voluptuous excitement he'd roused, the heady need that she'd surrendered to without any fear. And the tenderness with which he'd held her afterwards, the sleepy stroke of his hands across her sensitised skin, the safety she'd felt lying against him.

An agony of grief mingled with an abject fear. 'No,' she whispered.

Surely she hadn't been so foolish? This couldn't be love...

She dragged in a shaking breath. 'No,' she said firmly. She was not so stupid. So he was a fantastic lover. How many women had he bedded to be so proficient?

Hundreds, probably. 'Well, scores, anyway,' she told herself harshly.

But he'd understood her rejection, and he hadn't been disappointed by it, even though it might have been a bit of a shock.

The sound of her telephone was a welcome interruption to her tumbling thoughts.

'Oh, hello, Mrs Nixon,' she said, welcoming that familiar, friendly voice.

'Hello, dear, I haven't seen you for ages, apart from a word or two in the shop. Why don't we have lunch together at the café on the river and catch up on things? I'll pick you up and bring you home. How about Saturday and we can go to the market before we have lunch?'

Arrangements completed, Elana hung up, grateful to have something normal and everyday to look forward to. Count Niko Radcliffe had been taking up too much room in her mind. And lunch with Mrs Nixon was always fun. At least she'd catch up with all the local gossip and some international stuff too.

Until then, she'd avoid Niko as much as she could. And she wouldn't think of him.

Easier said than done, unfortunately. Although he spent much of the time she was at Mana out on the land with the farm manager, she couldn't avoid eating lunch with him, and often morning and afternoon tea. Always a stimulating companion, he treated her with a courtesy she found incredibly painful. Unfortunately, each occasion only reinforced her reckless longing for more than he could give her.

Elana despised herself for it. It was not only embarrassing, it was humiliating. She'd thought she'd been heartbroken when Roland had shown his true colours, but relief had overridden that. Now, however, every night when she fell into bed memories of bliss came crowding back, taking over her dreams. More than once she found herself waking, tears on her cheeks as she gulped back sobs.

'Stick it out,' she told herself grimly. 'It's only infatuation. Niko's certainly not pining for *you*.'

But she ached for him…an ever-present hunger that showed no sign of easing, an acute, savage need that refused to go away. The more time she shared with him, the more potent that longing became.

So lunch with Mrs Nixon was a welcome relief. The café overlooked the Falls, a wall of ancient solidified lava at the head of the estuary over which the river fell into a basin lined with mangrove trees. The sun gilded the moored yachts and launches bobbing gently in the current, and a salt tang mingled with the fresh scent of the native vegetation lining the low banks. Above the falls the river had scooped a pool, and from it came the happy shrieks of children swimming.

Without looking at the menu Mrs Nixon announced, 'I'm going to be completely sinful and have their superb fish and chips.'

The café's fish and chips came with salad and home-made mayonnaise, and were, as its publicity announced, world famous in Waipuna.

After they'd both ordered she leaned towards

Elana and said, 'And while we're waiting, you can tell me what you think of the Count now you know him.'

Elana hesitated, then made up her mind. 'Decisive, very astute, very self-contained, and with a proper appreciation of both Mana and the treasure trove of documents we've found there.'

And a superb lover...

Her companion nodded. 'Good. What do you think of his ideas for a kiwi conservation group on the peninsula?'

'I think it's excellent.' Elana told her of the impression the discovery of the last colony of takehe birds had made on Niko, and listened to the older woman's praise for his interest in the rapidly reducing kiwi population on the peninsula.

While they were waiting for the meal to arrive, Mrs Nixon said confidentially, 'You've given me your public views of Niko Radcliffe's character; now, for my ears only, what *do* you think of him?'

Elana laughed. 'Basically the same.' And counter-attacked. 'Anyway, you probably know more about him than I do. From information gathered from the gossip magazines in the dentist's surgery,' she elaborated.

Mrs Nixon's startled expression gave way to

amusement. 'Oh, I don't believe much more than half of that. Even the paparazzi don't seem to be able to keep tabs on him, but there are hints that he's been seeing some aristocrat in England.'

Pain seared through Elana. Probably the woman he'd sent flowers to.

'Apart from that,' Mrs Nixon went on, 'he's donated a lot of money to a conservation project in the Amazon somewhere.'

Elana wished he didn't have any good points. However, just because he spent largely on conservation projects didn't mean that she could ignore that hissed warning over the telephone.

Although the past few weeks had shown her a different side of Niko, she couldn't let herself believe anything about him that might persuade her to lower her defences. If she allowed herself to do that, she suspected it would be impossible to control her leashed emotions.

And apart from living next door to each other, and a certain sexual attraction, what had she and Niko in common?

Nothing.

'That's a strange look on your face,' Mrs Nixon observed, startling her.

Hastily composing her expression, she conjured up a smile. 'Is it? What sort of look?'

'Wistful, I think. Yes, wistful. And a little bit sad, too?'

'Mum used to love coming here.' Feeling like a coward for making use of her mother's memory, Elana went on briskly, 'And she'd be shocked to think just coming here would make me miserable. One thing she did was live every moment of her life to the full.'

'Yes, she did.' Unexpectedly, her companion patted Elana's hand. 'You've had a really hard time this past year. Fran and I have been worried about you.'

Touched, Elana said, 'You don't need to worry, you know. I'm managing.'

'I know.' She looked past Elana. 'Well, talk of the devil—guess who's coming in the door, and with a very elegant woman too. I wonder if this is the next woman in his life—although she looks a tad too old for him.'

Elana swallowed, the back of her neck prickling. Her companion smiled above Elana's head. 'Hello, Niko.'

'Mrs Nixon, Elana.'

Summoning a smile, Elana turned to meet Niko's

bland gaze. With him was the woman she'd seen beside him in the street.

'Let me introduce Petra Curtiss,' Niko said coolly. 'She is going to oversee the rescue of Mana's gardens.'

Mrs Nixon beamed. 'Oh, how wonderful. They used to be so lovely. Do you want to talk business, or would you like to share our table?'

Elana stiffened. Did she *have* to be so kind and hospitable?

But Niko said coolly, 'We've already talked business. Petra's on her way back to Auckland, and she'll probably be interested in any memories you have of the garden.'

Smiling at Mrs Nixon, the woman beside him said, 'I'd love to hear whatever you have to tell me about it.'

Niko nodded. 'Then we'll sit here,' he said smoothly, and held out the chair opposite Elana.

Which meant he'd be next to her. An exquisite tension gripped her, shredding her thoughts into irrational snippets as her heart skittered into overdrive. She had to force herself to smile when he sat down.

Relax, darn it! She focused on the conversation between the landscape architect and Mrs Nixon, who was very ready to discuss her memories of the garden.

Petra took notes, asked questions, apologised for monopolising the conversation, and impressed them all with her knowledge of plants that would flourish in a seaside garden.

'I grew up by the sea,' she explained. 'Just north of Auckland, so I have a good idea of what will grow up here and what won't.' She smiled across at Niko. 'I wouldn't be nearly so useful if you'd wanted me to rescue the garden at your high country station.'

'Fortunately that's in good shape,' he said urbanely. 'My father was a gardener rather than a farmer.'

An odd flatness in his tone caught Elana's attention. She glanced up, saw that he was looking at her, and her heart jumped in her chest, her pulse quickening, and her lips suddenly strangely hot and full.

Battling for control, she looked down at her meal.

'I was talking to young Jordan's mother the other day,' Mrs Nixon said, smiling at Niko. 'She told me you've been very helpful to him.'

'He's a decent kid at heart, and in a way the accident helped him grow up a bit. It certainly convinced him that he isn't bulletproof,' Niko said calmly.

'I believe he's working at Mana on the weekends?'

'He's saving up for a course on safe driving.' Niko sounded a little bored now, a tone that made Elana bristle.

Mrs Nixon smiled. 'In Auckland, I believe. You told him about that?'

'It seemed a logical thing to do,' Niko said dryly. 'I pointed out that if he wanted to drive fast he needed to know how and where to do it without killing himself or anyone else.' Smoothly changing the subject, he asked, 'Is that a dolphin I can see out there?'

'Oh, yes!' Elana scrambled to her feet, closely followed by Petra Curtiss.

The dolphin turned out to be two, a mother and a baby. Elana pointed them out, saying, 'I wonder why they're on their own.'

'I was wondering that too. They're usually in groups, aren't they?'

'Yes, the pods are family groups, so the babies are protected.'

'Do you often see them here?'

'Not here, no. Never, in fact. Ah, here come the rest.'

Entranced, they stood watching, rapidly joined by several other diners at the café, until eventually the pod of dolphins decided to leave.

Back at the table, Elana sensed a change in the atmosphere. Not one she could put her finger on, but both Mrs Nixon and Niko seemed different somehow, and although they finished their meal in pleasant conversation she still registered a coolness—mostly, she realised, from Niko.

When the meal finally finished she stifled a sigh of relief. Only to be shocked into near panic when Niko said smoothly, 'I'll take you home, Elana.'

'Oh, but—'

'It will save Mrs Nixon from going so far out of her way,' he said.

Mrs Nixon hesitated, almost as though she was reluctant to agree to this but unable to think of a polite way to stop it, before nodding. 'Very well. Thank you.'

Elana said, 'Thank you, Niko.' And smiled at Mrs Nixon. 'Thanks so much, it's been great fun.'

Farewells over, Mrs Nixon drove off, immediately followed by Petra Curtiss on her way back to Auckland.

As she and Niko walked towards his car, Elana said, 'It was kind of you to give Jordan something else to think about besides hooning around the back roads.'

Again that swift lift of broad shoulders. 'It's a stage in many young men's lives. He'll be fine. And the roads will be safer.'

She chuckled, then added more soberly, 'I hope so.'

'You should do that more often,' he said, stopping by the car to open the door for her.

Startled, she looked up. 'What?'

'Laugh,' he said succinctly. 'It's a pretty sound.'

Elana flushed. 'Thank you,' she murmured, climbing hastily into the front seat.

He walked around the car and got in, but instead of starting the engine he turned to face her. 'Hasn't anyone told you that before?'

'Not that I recall,' she said abruptly, strangely self-conscious. Relieved when he switched on the engine, she strapped herself into her seatbelt and gazed resolutely ahead as they headed back towards Mana, wondering at Niko's unexpected kindness to Jordan. No wonder the young man respected him.

It was probably naïve of her to be surprised—and warmed—by Niko's determination to introduce conservation to Mana. New Zealand farmers had come to realise just how fragile the ecosystem could be, and many were planting along stream banks. Then there was the kiwi restoration project he was working on with the other local landowners. He was a complex man, hard to read, clearly generous and charitably minded.

And she found it impossible to dismiss the memory of his tenderness during their lovemaking...

Even though, according to the woman who'd made that phone call, he was also capable of violence.

A chill ran down her spine.

'What's the matter?'

Niko's abrupt question startled her. 'Nothing,' she returned after a moment of hesitation. And couldn't stop herself from enquiring, 'Are you watching the road?'

His smile was sardonic. 'I am. I've also allowed myself the occasional glance at your profile. You've looked rather downcast since you got into the car.'

'I was thinking of Jordan,' she said, not entirely truthfully.

Why on earth should he be glancing at her? He'd accepted that she wasn't going to make love with him again. Obviously it didn't upset him.

'He'll be all right,' Niko said, his tone revealing complete conviction.

'I know. But occasionally I wonder what would have happened if we hadn't been driving home that night.'

'That's a waste of time.'

'I suppose it is.'

Niko glanced across at her profile—unreadable now, but she had to be thinking of those she had loved and lost in a car smash.

'How is it that Mrs Nixon seems to know everything that's happened in the district? Is she part of some hidden circle that keeps a close watch on everyone?'

'Ugh!' She shivered at the thought. 'No, there's no secret circle of gossipers in Waipuna. It's just that she was born and grew up here, she knows everybody, and she's so kind-hearted that people confide in her. You may have noticed she hasn't said an unkind word about anyone.'

'Is that why you told her we'd made love?'

She swivelled to stare at him, her expression freezing. 'I did not!' she said unevenly.

'Possibly she knows you so well she could guess.' He spoke in the toneless voice she hated, a voice that made it obvious he didn't believe her. 'While you and Petra were exclaiming at the dolphins in the bay, Mrs Nixon took the time to warn me—without actually coming out and saying it in so many words—that you are in a fragile state emotionally.'

Stunned, Elana stared at him. His face was unreadable, the strong lines and angles of his profile forbidding. 'Oh, for heaven's sake!' she said unevenly. 'So from that you assumed I'd opened my girlish heart to confide in her?'

Niko shrugged. 'She's obviously very fond of you, and you of her. Why?'

'Why am I fond of her? Because—'

Without ceremony he cut in, 'Why did you confide in her?'

She drew in a hard, sharp breath. Between her teeth she stated grittily, 'I did not confide anything. Why on earth would I?'

'How would I know?'

Seething, she said crisply, 'She knows me very well. Possibly she may have noticed a slight difference in my attitude to you, or yours to me, and drawn her own conclusions. I can assure you that I do not announce even to my closest friends who I've gone to bed with—especially when I'm regretting my stupidity.'

CHAPTER TEN

As soon as her angry words had left her lips, Elana regretted them. 'Oh, for crying out loud,' she blurted, 'I don't mean—well, you know how I was—afterwards, I mean.' She stopped, took a deep breath and went on more calmly, 'Niko, I wasn't casting aspersions on your prowess as a lover. I'm just regretting I allowed things to go so far.'

Niko negotiated a right-hand bend, then swung the wheel to avoid a large cattle truck taking up more than its share of the road. Elana gasped as the two vehicles passed each other with inches to spare.

Thanking fate that he was now familiar with the road, Niko eased over onto the narrow verge. Once the car had stopped he glanced sideways, took in Elana's colourless face and tightly clamped eyes, and swore silently.

She was shaking, white-knuckled hands clenched in her lap and her soft mouth trembling.

He reined in his temper, furious with himself and whatever benighted coincidence had seen to it that they'd met a truck right then.

Elana bit her lip, trying to regain control over her reaction. Her whole body ached, and she felt sick with the aftermath of a sudden flashback to the accident.

And then she felt a hand on hers, warm and strong. Very strong.

What next? she thought crazily, opening her eyes to stare straight ahead.

Niko said quietly, 'I'm sorry. Are you all right?'

She dragged in a quivering breath. 'I—yes.'

'You're shivering.' His hand tightened around hers. 'Of all the damned times to meet a truck…'

'I'm all right.' Until that truck appeared she'd been fine, buoyed into rudeness by an anger she now regretted. 'I'm sorry too,' she added lamely.

'You don't need to be.'

She let out a silent breath and tried to control her trembling body. Voice tight and controlled, she said, 'And I didn't mean what I said.'

He was silent for several heartbeats—a moment that seemed to drag unbearably. 'I accept that you didn't confide in Mrs Nixon. I made the wrong assumption, and I regret it.'

Startled, she glanced up at him. His face was carved from stone, austere and forceful, and to her surprise she found herself saying awkwardly, 'That's all right.'

His mouth relaxed and his sideways glance shimmered with amusement. 'I gather telling her to mind her own business wouldn't work?'

'I'm afraid not,' she said wryly, settling back into the seat as he set the car in motion again.

'I hope I managed to assuage her fears.'

Desperate to change the subject, Elana asked, 'Do you have lots of relatives?'

'Quite a few,' he told her dryly, slowing as they approached a sharp corner. 'Mostly on my mother's side, but cousins and an aunt on my father's. They live in the South Island.'

'Do you have any official position in San Mari?'

Immediately she wished she hadn't asked it. It was no business of hers.

However he didn't seem to think it an impertinence. 'As my mother's son, and a Count of the princedom, I have obligations. My presence is requested at important official occasions, and I have quarters at the palace when I stay there.'

Her pulse still jumping, Elana sat silently while they drove the last few kilometres. Quite a few relatives, and quite a few lovers, too…and at least one of them filled with vengeful regret.

The thought made her stupid heart ache. When the car drew up outside her house, she summoned all her self-control and said, 'Thanks for bringing me home.'

'I'll see you to the door,' he said brusquely.

Only to the door? Some reckless part of her chilled with desolation. *No,* she told herself angrily, *you do not want a repeat of the last time he was here.*

Not now, not ever again. Too dangerous by far. And what had seemed inevitable and *right* that night was, in the unforgiving light of hindsight, a shameful memory of her surrender to an uncontrolled and primitive impulse, a surrender so out of character she longed to push it to the furthest corner of her mind, to wipe it completely.

And knew she'd never be able to do that.

'Niko, you don't need to,' she said in what she hoped was a polite instead of fraught voice.

Without answering, he got out, and by the time she'd freed herself from the seatbelt he was opening her door.

And standing altogether too close.

'Thank you,' she said as she charged past him towards the front door, and sanctuary.

Please, just go, she begged silently as she scrabbled to unlock the door. *Before I lose it entirely and make a total idiot of myself.*

From behind, he said abruptly, 'Give me the key.'

'It's all right. I don't know why it's sticking.'

He reached out, and caught her wrist. 'What's the matter?'

'Let me go.'

Instantly he released her. In a different voice he said quietly, 'It's all right, Elana. Calm down.'

At last she got the key in the lock and twisted it, pushing the door open. She took a step into the house and forced herself to turn. He was frowning, his eyes narrowed and intent, his mouth a hard line.

'You are frightened,' he said quietly, stepping back. 'Why? Do you think I might hurt you?'

'Might you?' she demanded, before she had time to think.

He said frigidly, 'I do not hurt women.'

In spite of the telephone call, the utter disgust in his tone almost convinced her he was telling the truth. Too afraid to rely on it, she said, 'I'm not afraid of you.'

Not of him—she was scared of herself. Terrified, in fact. Because she was falling—falling in love with him...

Not only did she not trust him, she couldn't trust herself.

Still frowning, still with that intent, probing gaze, he said, 'Then what is this all about? Yes, I was irritated when I thought you might have confided to Mrs Nixon, but more *for* you than *with* you. Kind-hearted she may be, but she's a gossip. Small country towns are usually pretty conservative—'

'Her gossip is kind-hearted,' Elana said crisply. 'Even if she does suspect that we—that we—' Her mouth dried and her tongue wouldn't move.

'Made love,' he said curtly. 'That's what we did.'

She hurried on, 'Well, even if she suspects it she's not going to spread it around the district. Your reputation will be safe.'

Niko shrugged, his expression impossible to read. 'I don't care about my reputation. I do happen to care about yours.' He stopped. 'You look surprised.'

She was surprised. And strangely touched. Before she could answer he went on, 'You live here and will bear the brunt of gossip, if there is any. I don't want you to suffer for what happened between us.'

Did he too regret those impassioned hours in her bed?

If so, it wasn't nearly as much as she did, her conviction that she wouldn't fall in love with him echoing through her mind like a forlorn hope.

Yet surely this complex feeling—a mixture of fierce need and something else, something she yearned for—couldn't be love. It was too—too headstrong, too compelling...as though she had no control over it or herself any more.

If this was love, she'd never experienced it before.

It took every ounce of willpower to force her voice into steadiness. 'I won't suffer for it. Waipuna people might be conservative, but they won't throw me on a bonfire for indulging in premarital sex.'

And felt a kind of startled pleasure at the way his brows rose.

'Premarital sex?' he asked, in a tone that sent

248 CLAIMED BY HER BILLIONAIRE PROTECTOR

an erotic shiver the length of her spine. 'I prefer the term *making love* myself.'

And he reached for her, his arms closing around her in a grip that would have allowed her to break free easily.

Except that she didn't want to. She couldn't prevent a fiery hunger that should have added to her fears.

Instead it recharged her, infused her with a boldness that held her still in his embrace when he said softly, 'Tell me to go.'

'Why?'

Yes, that was her voice, low and soft.

And eager...

'Only if you want me to go,' Niko said, his voice husky.

'I don't.'

Somewhere, so far in the back of her mind that it had no power, a little voice whispered, *What are you doing?*

She shivered at the hard strength of his body against her, the way his arms tightened around her, as though she were something precious to him.

And then she recalled the hissed warning about his violence, and stiffened.

Instantly his arms loosened, and he stepped

back and surveyed her, eyes darkening as she lifted her head and met his gaze—cold, oh, so *cold*...

He said, 'No?'

It took all of her courage to say, 'I'm *sorry*—'

'You don't need to be,' he said, his voice hard. 'And stop looking so appalled—I'm going.'

Niko swivelled and walked away. *What the hell was going on here?*

She'd been like fire in his arms, her eyes smoky and half closed in invitation, her mouth softening in eager anticipation. And then so quickly it had shocked him, that voluptuous surrender had been replaced by something that looked ominously close to panic.

Why? When they'd made love there had been no fear in her, nothing but an ecstatic surrender that had haunted him since.

The thought that she might be afraid appalled him. Had she read something in the media that made her wonder about him? For the first time he found himself regretting his previous lovers. His emotions were churning in a turmoil of astonishment and anger—and something else, a feeling he'd never experienced before. He needed time to work out what was happening.

* * *

Elana watched him leave, something cracking painfully inside her. A fierce longing weakened her as his vehicle disappeared around the corner. Turning, she found her way into the house, tears gathering so thickly she had to stop and wipe them away before she could close the door behind her and relax into the silence and familiarity of her home.

Always before the house had meant comfort and safety, but now it seemed alien, a place that held only memories of a life not of her making.

She made herself a cup of tea and sat down with it on the deck, staring sightlessly over the calm waters of the estuary as she told herself she'd done the right thing.

Making love with Niko had been—beyond wonderful. And intensely dangerous.

Thankfully, she'd been able to summon the strength to stick to her decision not to continue being his New Zealand lover. Painfully she wondered how she'd summoned the courage to do it.

And as she drew on her reserves of courage, she found herself wondering if perhaps the woman who'd told her he could be violent might—just *might*—have been trying to cause mischief.

Because each time she'd said no, Niko had accepted her refusal with cool equanimity and no sign of anger. Either the urge to violence was not in his repertoire of emotions, or he was able to control any impulse to hurt when it suited him.

Which?

Tomorrow she'd have to go to Mana and continue work on the documents. Niko would be there. How would he greet her? And why, oh, *why* was she feeling as though all that was good in her life had come to an end?

She'd never felt like this before. Not even when she'd thought she'd been in love with Roland, when she'd allowed herself to dream of a life with him, only to have those dreams dashed.

Compared to the emotions that gripped her now, her previous affair had been pale and emotionless.

Below on the beach a gull called, the shrill sound cutting through the soft purr of tiny waves. She tried to draw strength from the familiarity— the glorious dazzle of sunlight on the water, its golden swathe covering the hills on the other side of the estuary.

No strength came. But it would, she promised herself as she drained her teacup and walked inside. It was totally unfair of fate to dangle such temptation before her, but at least she'd had the strength to resist.

Not that it improved her mood. In the end she set herself to scouring out a cupboard, and then went out into the garden to pull weeds from amongst the vivid clump of valotta bulbs. They'd been her mother's favourite flowers; she'd loved the luminously scarlet flowers fired by sunlight that bloomed when most summer flowers were fading.

The shrill call of the telephone summoned her inside. She arrived there puffing, only to have the breath stop in her throat when she heard Niko's voice.

'I'm leaving shortly,' he said crisply. 'I don't know how long I'll be away. How far have you actually got with the transcribing of documents?'

Trying to match his businesslike tone, she replied, 'I estimate there's about a month's work left. Possibly six weeks, unless we find any more.'

'I'll be in touch. If you need to contact me about anything, email me, OK? Goodbye, Elana.'

'Goodbye, Niko. Travel safely.'

Heart knotting painfully in her chest, Elana hung up.

So that was it. Goodbye.

He'd been totally cool, his voice emotionless, making sure she understood that he'd accepted her decision not to further their relationship.

It was what she wanted—sensible, safe.

But oh, it *hurt*. She had to blink back an onslaught of weak tears.

Well, she'd been hurt before, and got over it. She'd cope. A few hours with a sexy billionaire meant absolutely nothing in the total scheme of things.

Nothing.

Yet during the following weeks Elana felt she was sleepwalking through her life. Fortunately, apart from Mrs Nixon, who asked her anxiously several times if she was entirely well, nobody seemed to notice. Life plodded on while she worked on the Mana documents, arranged flowers in the shop, wrote articles on historic churches in Northland for a magazine, gardened, and endured the grey weeks as they dragged past.

Each night she promised herself that this would be the night she no longer dreamed of Niko Radcliffe, only to wake in the mornings with tears on her cheeks. She and Niko communicated, but each time she saw him on the screen it twisted her heart.

Fran visited, insisting on staying with her for several nights, and told her she needed to eat more and get out into the sun. 'Pale and ethereal is OK, pale and wan is most definitely *not*,' she'd said firmly. 'And you've lost weight.'

'I have not.'

'Well, you look as though you have. What's the matter? Are you in love? Is it not going well?'

Fran's sensible attitude would probably be helpful, but for once, Elana couldn't confide in her. 'I'm fine,' she said stoutly. 'I've been busy—and being shut inside with a stack of old documents is not conducive to getting a decent tan, which is something I've never managed to achieve in my life, as you well know.'

'No, you just go a lovely soft gold colour,' Fran said enviously. She eyed Elana. 'OK, so you're not talking, but you'd better start looking more cheerful or Mum will take you in hand.'

Both touched and irritated, Elana managed a smile. 'I'm shaking already,' she said.

They both laughed, and to her relief Fran said no more.

Once she'd left, Elana admitted to herself that her heart might be suffering—well, perhaps even cracked. But not broken. A one-night stand, however ecstatic, did not—*could* not—mean she'd fallen in love with Niko Radcliffe.

Surely the longer he stayed away, the easier it would be to conquer this painful longing.

Nobody had mentioned a date for his return, and she wasn't going to ask. When she'd finished the documents at Mana she'd no longer be constantly reminded of Niko.

On the day the schoolchildren arrived to plant more shrubs and trees on the creek banks, now all fenced off from cattle, Patty West met her at the door of the homestead. Smiling, Elana joined her in waving as the small bus went by with a toot and much waving of hands.

'I'd better get to work too,' Elana said. 'Not much longer for me here, either. I'm nearly finished.'

'We'll miss you.' The older woman looked up at the sound of another engine. 'Good, here comes my man. He's got a doctor's appointment and I've got some shopping to do. We'll be back by lunchtime, though.'

'Do you want me to take any calls?'

'I don't think there'll be any, but if you could, thank you.'

An hour later Elana lifted her head as the telephone rang imperatively. 'Mana Station,' she said into the receiver.

'Elana, it's Rangi Moore—the teacher with the planting group.' He sounded harassed. 'I've got a girl here who's not feeling well—she says she's not feeling sick, but I think she almost fainted, and she's certainly very pale. I can't leave the rest of the group on their own, and I can't contact her parents, so can you ask one of the Wests to come and get her, and—wait a minute. Yes, Sarah?'

Elana waited for a few seconds before he said, 'Her parents had to go to see the accountant in Whangarei today. Sarah doesn't know which firm, and her mother's cell phone is turned off. The heat here is really getting to her. If Mrs West could look after her—'

'The Wests aren't here right now, but it's OK, I'll come and collect Sarah. She can come home with me and you can pick her up from my place on your way back to school.'

'That would be great,' he said, clearly relieved. Then, in a different tone, 'Actually, perhaps you should keep her at the homestead? Her parents know we're here. Do they know you?'

Elana blenched. The prospect of managing a sick child in one of the homestead's gloriously rejuvenated rooms was momentarily terrifying until she recalled the loungers out on the veranda. Tucked into one of those in the shade of the grapevine, the girl would be cool and the rooms would be safe. 'No, I don't know them at all, so, OK, the homestead's probably a better idea.'

'You know where we are?'

She glanced out of the window. 'I can see you from here. You're in the gully by the pump shed. I'll be there shortly.'

By the time she arrived in her car both child and teacher were waiting for her. Tall for her twelve or so years and clutching her school bag as though it were a lifeline, the girl had lost all her colour, the freckles on her face standing out like tiny copper coins.

'Hop in,' Elana said, hoping she made it back to the homestead without any untoward incident. Sarah clambered silently into the front seat and remained silent, her eyes closed, while they drove back to the homestead.

Elana switched off the engine. 'Sarah, stay there,' she said, afraid the girl was going to faint. She opened the door and helped Sarah out, catching her as she staggered.

Straightening up, the girl whispered, 'I want to go home.'

Elana hugged her. 'I'm sorry, but we can't contact your parents. As soon as we can, we'll organise things better for you.' She steered her up the steps onto the veranda and towards the lounger. 'Sit there in the shade. I'll get you a pillow and a glass of water.'

Sarah shuddered. 'I don't want a drink, thank you,' she said in a small voice, and almost fell onto the lounger. She lay back and closed her eyes. 'My head's hurting.'

'I'll see if I can get you something to ease it. Have you had headaches before?'

Sarah nodded. 'Mum gives me an aspirin.'

'I've got aspirin in my bag. I'll be back shortly.'

By the time she arrived back with a glass of water, Sarah had regained some colour. She drank the water and swallowed the aspirin, then opened her eyes. 'I can hear a plane—no—a helicopter.'

A sudden rush of delight took Elana by surprise. 'If it's a helicopter it will be Mr Radcliffe,' she said quietly.

Sarah managed a pale smile. 'I like him. Everyone does. He's nice.'

Nice? If she hadn't been so anxious about the

girl Elana could have laughed at that description. Niko could be kind, he was certainly protective, and he was a fantastic lover. But nice...?
She steadied her voice and said, 'You're looking a bit better now. How's your head?'

'Still banging.' Sarah closed her eyes, but opened them when the helicopter descended onto the landing pad.

Elana kept her gaze on her as she watched it land. Although she was still pale as a wraith, the landing was giving the girl something other to think of than her misbehaving body.

Once the rotors eased back and the noise began to die away, Sarah asked, 'Does Mr Radcliffe fly it himself?'

'I don't know,' Elana said, adding, 'You can ask him—if it is him.'

Sarah said, 'Yes.' And after a moment in a slightly stronger voice, 'Yes, I will.'

Tension tightened Elana's nerves as the chopper door opened and Niko climbed out, a bag in his hand. He strode towards the house, altering direction when he saw them on the veranda.

A swift rush of adrenalin powered through her, filling her with a forbidden, intense delight. Realisation hit her with immense force.

She loved this man. She would love him for ever. If only she could trust him...

He stopped beneath the balustrade and looked at them. 'What's the matter, Sarah?'

Startled, Elana wondered if he knew all of the children by name.

Sarah managed another half-smile and staggered up from the lounger. 'I feel sick.' After a second adding miserably, 'And my head hurts.'

He nodded and stepped up onto the veranda. 'Close your eyes and see if that makes you feel better while Elana and I go inside so she can tell me about it.'

'I think—' Sarah gagged, clapping her hand over her mouth.

Too late. To Elana's horror the child threw up all over Niko, and then burst into tears, shaking uncontrollably.

Niko reached out and patted her shoulder. In a calm, bracing tone, he soothed, 'It's all right, don't worry about it. Elana will take you to the bathroom.'

Stunned, Elana said, 'Come on, Sarah. You'll feel a lot better once you wash your face.'

'There's a shower room inside the back door,' Niko said.

Elana nodded and took the sobbing girl's hand, steering her along the veranda. Once in the bathroom she provided her with a warm wet face flannel and a glass.

'Just rinse your mouth out with water,' she told Sarah, who was still crying softly.

That done, she checked the girl's clothes, fortunately unaffected by the bout of nausea, before taking her out and coaxing her to lie on another lounger. Once settled, she asked, 'Do you feel at all better?'

'A b-bit.' Sarah opened her eyes to give Elana a scared look. 'I hope he isn't mad at me,' she whispered.

'He won't be,' Elana said, and realised with some shock that she was certain of it.

Why? Because of his calmness and control? Into her mind there flashed the memory of an incident just after she'd started school. She'd been so proud of being trusted to carry a glass of milk for herself, only to trip and tip it over her father. His reaction was seared into her brain. He'd been icily furious, blaming her mother for being stupid enough to give her a glass of milk in the first place, then stripping Elana of all her pride and her confidence.

She'd actually braced herself for a similar reaction from Niko.

And yet, although his response had startled her, deep inside she'd *known* that he wouldn't react as her father had.

Which meant—*what*? What sort of man *was* Niko Radcliffe? Dared she even consider that he might be a man she could respect? A man she could safely allow herself to love?

Be sensible, she told herself curtly, every word of the unknown woman's warning etched into her brain. Tender and considerate he might have been when they'd made love—and then fiercely and intoxicatingly exciting—but that meant only that he'd had plenty of experience.

She walked across to the balustrade and stood for long moments staring into the sunburst of colour from a mass of daisies in the garden beneath.

A slight sound behind her made her turn. But it wasn't Sarah. She'd dropped off to sleep and the colour was coming back into her cheeks.

It was Niko, clearly showered and in clean clothes, and carrying a shirt in his hand. He surveyed Sarah and smiled. 'I got this just in case, but I see it's not necessary.'

'No, fortunately her clothes escaped the on-slaught.'

'Poor kid.'

Sarah stirred, her lashes fluttering, and opened her eyes to direct a startled, shamed look at Niko.

He said, 'You look much better. How do you feel now?'

'M-much better.' She hesitated then blurted, 'I'm so sorry—I didn't mean to—I—I couldn't—'

Niko interrupted, 'Sarah, it's all right. These things happen, and there's nothing you could do about it. I'm very glad you're feeling much better. Stop worrying, OK?'

She gave him a shy smile. 'OK.'

'Good girl.' He transferred his gaze to Elana. 'Where's Patty?'

Elana glanced at her watch. 'She's in Waipuna, but she should be back pretty soon—before lunch,' she said.'

'Any minute then,' he said, and looked down at her, smiling. 'And thanks.'

Strangely touched by his smile, she said un-steadily, 'No need for thanks. Now, I think we should try to get Sarah's mum on her cell phone again.'

But it was still turned off. Elana left another

message, and hoped that it wouldn't be too long before the woman called back. Without being coaxed, Sarah swallowed a small amount of water, and then went back to sleep.

She woke when Patty West arrived back— clearly surprised to see Niko—and while the housekeeper and Elana were preparing lunch, she sat talking to Niko as though she'd known him all her life, a talk only interrupted by the arrival of the schoolteacher and his group of tree-planting students.

After a swift inspection of the girl the teacher said, 'Thanks a million, Elana, for taking care of her. And thank you, Mr Radcliffe, for being so forbearing.'

Niko shrugged, smiled and held out his hand. 'It was nothing. And my name is Niko.'

Rangi smiled as they shook hands, then turned to look at his charge. 'She looks good enough to be able to come with us now and stay in the sick bay at school until her parents collect her.' He called her over and asked, 'Do you think you can cope with coming to school with us in the bus?'

Sarah looked torn, then nodded. 'I feel all right now,' she said a little shyly, adding, 'Actually, I feel a bit hungry.'

'Better wait until we get to school before you eat anything,' Rangi advised her. He thanked everyone, rounded up his group and shepherded the children into the bus then gave Elana a hug. 'And thank you, Elana, for taking over. See you around.'

The departure of the bus left Elana feeling oddly ill at ease. Niko remained silent as the sound of the engine died away. She glanced up, met cool blue eyes in a face more angular than usual, and said, 'I'd better be off too, and let you get settled.' And added, 'I didn't know you were coming back today.'

CHAPTER ELEVEN

'I WASN'T.' As though the words were torn from him Niko said, 'I had no intention of coming back so soon, but while I was away I discovered something.'

'What?' Elana asked, wondering. 'What did you discover?'

He paused, blue gaze hooded and unreadable. 'Once—after I told you that I was a citizen of both New Zealand and San Mari—you said that it meant I had two places to call home.'

Heart pounding, she nodded, her gaze fixed onto his hard, handsome face. 'I remember.' *I remember everything you ever said to me...*

'I was amused, because neither of them have ever seemed like home.' He paused, then added, 'In fact, I'd never had a place I thought of as home. The palace was huge and cold and impersonal, and my mother made travelling the globe her hobby. Usually without me. Then, when I was eight I went to boarding school.'

Her heart twisted. He must have understood her shocked response because he shrugged. 'Actually, I enjoyed it, but I certainly didn't call it home— nor did I consider the universities I attended to be homes. I spent some of the holidays with my father, but he lived like a bachelor, and for some time we were both wary of each other. We did find some common ground eventually.'

'I'm glad,' she said quietly, neither her expression nor her voice giving away her emotions.

Niko walked across the veranda and stared out over the much tidier garden for a moment, before turning to face her. He was finding this incredibly difficult, but he needed to tell her what he meant.

Calling on an icy control, he said in a clipped, hard voice, 'While I was away this time I discovered that you—that you mean home to me.'

The words jangled meaninglessly around her brain. She swallowed and croaked, 'What—what are you saying?'

His smile held no humour, and he didn't move. 'I have no idea how it happened, or when—but wherever you are is more home to me than any of the houses I own, either of the two countries I am a citizen of.'

Hope and a fearful happiness burst into flame in her heart. 'Niko, I don't understand.'

'It's quite simple. When I left Mana I finally discovered what love is,' he said, blue gaze fixed on her face. 'It's missing someone so intensely that you dream of them...'

All colour left her skin. Dumbly, eyes more gold than green, she nodded.

He took a step towards her, ready to catch her if she should faint. 'Ah, so you already know that,' he said harshly.

Her lips trembled and he waited, but no words came.

He resumed, 'And it's remembering little unimportant things—the way you lift your chin when you're telling me you don't need looking after, your laughter, refusing to have whisky in your tea after Jordan's accident, the warmth of your skin when we made love, the sound of your voice...'

He paused, but she still didn't speak. 'That's when I realised that every time I thought about returning to Mana my spirits lifted enormously.' He stopped, hard blue gaze kindling. 'Because you are here.'

A stunned, disbelieving joy held Elana prisoner. She stared at him, wondering if he meant it, but could find no words to answer. At the back of her mind was fear—a fear she had to deal with.

Still Niko didn't move. Harshly he said, 'Each time we spoke together on the computer, each time I saw you on the screen, I missed you more. I know that missing you every second of every day that I'm away from you is going to be part of my life from now on. I've never felt like that before, and it scares the hell out of me.'

'Scares you?' she whispered, and shook her head. 'I can't believe—'

'Believe it,' he broke in, his voice rough with emotion. 'I want to be with you—wherever you are—because without you my life will lose most of its meaning.'

Elana closed her eyes against the fears rioting through her mind. Did she have the courage to trust the instinct that told her he was no abuser? Memories of him—of his kindness, of consideration, of the times he'd helped her—were they enough?

Quietly he said, 'There's something you're afraid of. What is it, Elana? Do you think I'm like your father? Tell me what it is and we'll work it out together.'

After swallowing to ease her parched throat she

said hoarsely, 'My father—how did you know about him?'

His smile was filled with irony. 'Mrs Nixon, who else? Your mother confided in her.'

Shocked and sickened, she felt the heat drain from her face. 'Why—?' Gripped by an intense sensation of betrayal, she couldn't go on.

He shrugged. 'She saw more than I gave her credit for. She thought I should know. And she was right.'

'But *why*?'

He paused, then said roughly, 'I suspect she was worried that I might hurt you. I'm very grateful to her. We might have gone on misunderstanding each other for months if she hadn't warned me. What was your father like?'

She swallowed. 'He hit my mother.'

Niko's shock was followed by disgust and a cold rage that threatened to overwhelm him. 'Did he beat you?'

'No. But I knew what he was doing. I was terrified of him.'

He said something in what must have been the language of San Mari. 'How long did this go on for?'

'My mother ran away with me when I was five.

But he found us about a month later, and came after us and hauled me into the car. My mother rang the police but—he rammed the car into a tree. He was killed. I had a broken arm, but I was all right apart from that.' She shivered. 'He was going to kill me. He knew that would be the worst thing he could do to my mother.'

Niko fought back horror. 'His own child,' he said quietly. And before she could answer, he went on, 'I am so sorry that you had to endure such terror.'

Wild thoughts jostled through her mind. She said indistinctly, 'And then I stupidly had a bad experience with a man a couple of years ago.'

'You need to sit down.' He spoke between his teeth, cursed by a jealousy so fierce he couldn't say more, then pulled a chair out and held it while she automatically obeyed. Lowering himself onto the sofa, he asked, 'Do you want to talk about it?'

She sent him an astonished glance. 'No, but at least he wasn't physically abusive. I thought I loved him, but he was—he was a control freak. I got tired of being ordered about and treated like a halfwit. I had to tell him where I was all the time, he expected me to do what I was told.'

Niko shook his head. 'Trusting a man must

be very difficult for you. If I'd known, I'd have been more understanding.' He got up and walked across to the window, silhouetted against the luminous light outside. Without turning around he said, 'I knew you'd do a good job of working with the Mana documents, but I offered you the job mainly because I couldn't get you out of my head.'

Elana heard the words, but couldn't make sense of them. He turned, and she stared into his face, honed into arrogant angles as though what he was saying was bitter punishment.

Abruptly he said, 'At first I was certain it was lust—simple, basic, easily controlled.'

He stopped as though expecting her to say something, but no words came to her tongue. She didn't dare believe she'd heard correctly.

Resuming, his voice harsh, he said, 'I assumed that the hunger would go away, that familiarity would breed—oh, not contempt, never that—but boredom. Because that's what's happened before.' His smile held no humour. 'I thought I was like my mother. She fell quickly and easily in love, and out of it just as quickly, just as easily. When I was young I had the misfortune to catch the eye of the sister of one of my friends. It became embarrassing, and in the end I had to tell her that I didn't love her, that we were too young to even think of marrying. She tried to commit suicide.'

Elana braced herself. She didn't want to hear this—hated the thought of it, but she realised it was important to him.

'She didn't succeed, thank the saints, and is now happily married,' he continued, still in that level, emotionless voice. 'I decided I was too much like my mother to be trusted with the emotions of anyone innocent and unsophisticated. But the first time I saw you I wanted you. And every time I saw you it got stronger. And my emotions changed in ways I'd never experienced before.'

Stunned, Elana told him, 'I'm not so young, and I don't consider myself unsophisticated.'

'So if I'd suggested an affair with you—one without marriage—you'd have accepted?'

He waited while she digested this. For the first time in his life he was desperately afraid. Her face was expressionless, and she ran a shaky hand through her bright hair as she met his gaze, her green-gold gaze veiled by long lashes.

When she finally answered her voice was thin. 'No,' she admitted, her painful reluctance obvious. 'I was too afraid. As you said, I don't trust easily.'

He nodded. 'Then we made love. And—it was—it was new and shining and—something I'd never experienced. And I was elated because it was good for you too. Only afterwards you were bluntly clear that you had no intention of furthering our relationship. Yet even then I kept hoping that you'd relent.'

He waited as though expecting an answer, but she couldn't find any words. In the end he said, 'When Mrs Nixon confided in me about your father, I began to understand, but I didn't know how to deal with the situation. And I didn't know exactly what I felt for you. I intended to stay away for at least six months and do some serious thinking. But I missed you.' He paused, then went on harshly, 'Hell, that's such a *stupid* term. *Missed* you—I ached for you, I longed for you, I recalled every word you'd ever said to me, I looked forward to our talks on the VOIP with eagerness, and I dreamed of you when I slept.'

'But you were already with—' She stopped, and drew in a deep breath, then finishing, 'You had a partner when you came here. You sent her flowers—'

'They were a farewell gesture; we'd already broken up. And I broke it off because I'd met you. I cursed the fact that you were in the shop that day, but in a way I was relieved. I had never felt like that before, and I resented it.' He paused. 'You did too, didn't you?'

'I—well, yes.' And because he was being honest with her, she confessed, 'I suppose I used that, and—something else—as a buffer, a reason not to—'

After several seconds, he said quietly, 'Tell me, Elana. A reason not to do what?'

She realised her hands were twisting together, and stilled them. Although she didn't know what he was offering, and didn't know whether or not she dared accept it, she knew she had to be honest.

'Not to fall for you,' she said harshly. 'Not to trust you.'

'Was it so hard?'

'I—yes.'

He said, 'I can understand your fear. But I don't know how to deal with it. I can promise you that

I am no abuser, but how can I expect you to take my word for it?'

'It's not just that,' she said hoarsely.

'Then what?' He paused, then said harshly, 'If you want me to get out of your life, tell me now.'

Her eyes filled with tears. She turned away to hide them, and was instantly enveloped in his arms, held against his strength, his voice reverberating in her ears as he said, 'Tell me, Elana.'

She muttered, 'It—I don't know that I can.' Then drew in a breath. 'All right.'

And told him of the telephone call she'd taken. His arms didn't loosen, and she felt every muscle in his body tighten as she spoke of the woman who'd told her he could be violent.

When her voice died away he was silent for long moments. Tensely she waited.

After what seemed an eon he said quietly, 'I know who that was. When we broke up she threatened to go to the press with accusations of violence unless I paid her off. I told her I'd sue if she did.'

His arms dropped and he took a step back, eyes hard and a muscle flicking beside his jaw.

Chilled, Elana stared up into a face devoid of expression.

Bleakly he said, 'With your family history I understand why you find it difficult to trust. I can't prove that I'm not a violent man. Just as she can't prove that I am. I can only hope that you know me well enough to trust me.'

'But I don't know you very well at all,' she protested. And then caught her breath. 'And you don't really know me. I—I wouldn't fit into your life.'

'Why do you say that? You fit perfectly into my life.'

'This isn't your real life,' she said on a half-sob.

'Of course it is.' He took a step towards her, then stopped. In a raw voice he said, 'I won't touch you. *You* must make this decision.'

Wrenched by conflicting emotions, she stared at him, her heart in her eyes. 'I don't—I can't believe that you want me.'

'Believe it,' he said tersely. 'I want you, and I love you. I don't know how it happened, or even why, and believe me, I resisted it. But I know now that it's love. I must have fallen in love with you that first night at the ball. You were so brave when we came upon young Jordan, and you gave him every encouragement. I was impressed. And I was jealous of your policeman friend—stupidly.' He paused. 'Elana, if this isn't love, I don't know what is. I do know that it's driving me crazy. If you don't want this from me, tell me now and I'll go and never come back.'

Heart aching, so tense she couldn't formulate any words, she watched him turn away, until his name broke from her lips.

He stopped. For several seconds her future weighed heavily on her, until she gained the courage to say, 'Niko, wait—'

He swung around, and looked at her, nakedly importunate. 'Your decision,' he said.

And in that moment she knew. 'Don't go,' she said, and took a step towards him.

He froze. 'You're sure?'

On another half-sob she whispered, 'I'm not sure of anything, but I'm not a coward either.'

'Far from it,' he said, his voice tender, and reached for her. 'I swore I wouldn't do this, that it wouldn't be fair, but I can't—I don't—' he said roughly, then kissed her, gently at first, followed by kisses of such sweet fierceness that an answering wildness leaped up within her and she responded without fear, with no thought but for this passionate delight.

Finally he lifted his head, and looked down, eyes gleaming, his expression taut, and held her for long moments until her heart eased into a regular beat. When her breathing steadied, he said, 'Elana?'

She said clumsily, 'I love the way you say my name. And I love you.'

'I know that,' he said, and laughed when she lifted her head and fixed him with what she hoped was an indignant glare.

He sobered, and released her, but didn't step away. 'It's a matter of trust for both of us,' he said quietly. 'My parents' marriage wasn't a good model. I think my father loved my mother until he died. There were no other women in his life. But she couldn't cope with his life.'

'That's so sad,' Elana whispered.

'She decided she wasn't suited to marriage, so after she left him she had affairs.' He shrugged. 'And I've spent a fair amount of my adult life fending off women who look at me and see money, with all its benefits. You didn't.'

'How do you know?'

He was silent a moment. Then he said, 'I knew from the first that you were very aware of me. But always there was a barrier, a reserve. You weren't casting any lures. And cynic that I am, I wondered if that was a clever move on your part to whet my appetite. Then we made love.'

Elana drew a sharp breath and held it.

'It blew my mind.' He paused, that humourless smile playing around his lips. 'And then you made it obvious you weren't going to repeat it. You still stayed aloof, and I wondered again if you were just a little more clever than most of my other would-be lovers.' On a steely note he stated, 'Who were not as many as Mrs Nixon's gossip magazine writers suggest.'

'I'm glad,' she muttered, still bewildered by his confession, torn between intense joy and a deep-seated fear.

'I got an indication of the reason you were so distant that day at the restaurant when you and Petra watched the dolphins, and Mrs Nixon warned me off.'

She nodded, but couldn't find the right words to reply, and he continued, 'She clearly felt it was important. So I had your past checked out.'

Elana stiffened, and wrenched herself free, fixing him with a smouldering glare. 'And what,' she enquired starkly, 'did you find out?'

'Basically what you told me. That you and your

mother spent time in a refuge after she left him, and that he was killed driving away with you.'

She shivered at the harshness of his tone, and he reached for her. Voice deep and sure, he said, 'I can't promise to be the perfect husband, but—what's the matter?'

'Husband?' Stunned, she closed her eyes. 'I don't—'

Niko made a muffled noise that could have been a laugh or a groan. Or a combination of both. 'I'm making a total mess of this.' His voice deepened. 'Bear with me, please—it's the first time I've ever proposed to anyone, and it will be the last. I love you, Elana. I want you to be my wife, I want to be your husband. I want to make love with you, make delectable babies with you, quarrel with you, listen to you laugh every day and hear you breathing beside me every night. I want to show you my father's station in the South Island, and as many takehe birds as you want to see. I want us to celebrate anniversaries and buy each other fabulous presents. But more than anything, I hope you want those things too.' He paused a second, before adding, 'If you do happen to want all those things, then please put both of us out of our misery.'

She choked on a laugh mingled with a burst of tears, and whispered, 'Yes.'

'Yes what?'

'Yes to everything.'

And at last he kissed her, and she knew that she trusted him, loved him, would always love him and that she need have no fears for their future together.

EPILOGUE

'PANIA, SWEETHEART, TRY not to make so much noise.' Elana dropped a kiss on her daughter's nose, and was rewarded by a chuckle and a kiss on her own chin.

'But I'm the birthday girl, I'm seven years old today,' Pania said pertly. 'I'm allowed to be happy.'

'Happiness can be quiet, you know, and any more of that yelling is only going to wake the baby, and you know what will happen then.'

'Crying—lots of it,' Pania's brother Kent stated succinctly, ruffling her crown of blonde hair. 'And anyway, you're still a baby, Pania. I'm nearly nine.'

'You're only eight years and a half,' his sister asserted, pulling a face at him. 'When is Daddy coming? Does he know it's my birthday today?'

'Of course he does. He should arrive—' Elana stopped. 'Ah yes, what can I hear?'

Pania gave another squeal of pure joy, and ran

to the window with the best view of the landing pad. 'It's the helichopper! Look, look, there it is.'

Both children peered across the garden, watching the helicopter as it landed, then raced from the room and down the stairs. Elana waited a moment, and when no wail emanated from the baby's crib she followed them.

Niko had been busy for the past week at what was now his head office in Auckland, organising everything so their holiday at Mana would be uninterrupted.

She walked across the lawn towards the gate, noting that Kent grabbed Pania's hand before they reached it so she couldn't speed through into the forbidden landing pad. He was already showing signs of being every bit as protective—and autocratic—as his father.

And Pania, with her head of bright hair and her soft heart, reminded her sometimes of her mother. Their little Cara, five months old, was an unexpected gift. She had Niko's black hair and startlingly blue eyes.

Smiling, Elana watched as he got down from the helicopter and strode towards them.

Ten years previously she'd put all her trust in her instinct and her love for him. And she'd never regretted it. He'd shown her how magnificent a marriage of loving hearts could be.

He came towards her, a child hanging from each hand, his face alight with pleasure. 'Elana, darling girl, it's good to be back home,' he said, and kissed her.

Hand in hand they walked back to the homestead, and into their future, the future they had made together.

* * * * *

LET'S TALK
Romance

For exclusive extracts, competitions
and special offers, find us online:

f facebook.com/millsandboon

⊙ @millsandboonuk

🐦 @millsandboon

Or get in touch on 0844 844 1351*

For all the latest titles coming soon,
visit millsandboon.co.uk/nextmonth